Delhi: Anything Goes

Anita Kumar

Om Books International

First published in 2015 by

Om Books International

Corporate & Editorial Office
A-12, Sector 64, Noida 201 301
Uttar Pradesh, India
Phone: +91 120 477 4100
Email: editorial@ombooks.com
Website: www.ombooksinternational.com

Sales Office
107, Ansari Road, Darya Ganj,
New Delhi 110 002, India
Phone: +91 11 2326 3363, 2326 5303, 4000 9000
Fax: +91 11 2327 8091
Email: sales@ombooks.com
Website: www.ombooks.com

Text copyright © Anita Kumar

ISBN: 978-93-83202-22-5

Printed in India

10 9 8 7 6 5 4 3 2 1

To Mum And Dad,

My Daughters,

Anishka And Sonakshi,

And

To my *Guruji*

For His Eternal Grace And Blessings

Acknowledgements

I would like to thank my publisher and friend, Ajay Mago, and chief editor, Dipa Chaudhuri, of Om Books International, for believing in this book, my daughters, Anishka and Sonakshi, for their continued support and my family and friends for their encouragement — that includes my dear sisters-in-law Rittu, Selena and Kajal Kumar, my brothers Sanjeev Kumar, Ajay Bijli, Rajan and Sanjay Kumar, and my friends Bonnie Hazuria, Vikas Malhotra, R.P. Sharma, Sumi Kumar, Vernaz Mittal, Seema Jajodia and my soul brother, Vikram Baidyanath.

A special thanks to my friend, Sangeeta Dutta, for her invaluable inputs. Above all, I am deeply indebted to my Mom and my Dad and my Guruji for His eternal love and blessings.

Acknowledgements

Prologue

Delhi is commendably rich in many aspects; its monuments, its temples, the unstoppable development of shopping malls and the influx of many multinational companies setting up their business here. Its growing population makes it one of the fastest growing cities in the world; so it is as multi-cultural as it is multi-lingual. Therefore, the city represents a mindset that is as diverse as its burgeoning population.

The fast evolving city has not only absorbed the diversity of its population, it has also opened its doors to the Western culture with its exposure to foreign trade, foreign goods, satellite TV and foreign people; so much so that nothing in Delhi is foreign anymore besides perhaps its own traditional mindset. The city, particularly the high society, has, quite willingly, imported a certain cultural sensibility that was once looked upon with awe.

However, this so called progressive mindset is somewhat vacuous in the fact that it has eroded a certain value system that once lent the city its redolent charm. The effects of this change are most apparent in the city's social scene, which is witnessing an upsurge of the nouveau riche; a society that is characterised by pomposity and display of wealth. So, it is not unusual to overhear conversations peppered with brand names like, Chanel, Hermes, Gucci and Prada or overhear a mellifluous voice say, 'The Kapoors flew in Usher so we will fly in Lady Gaga' or 'Its Silver Tips Imperial tea and botox this afternoon and Beluga caviar and cocaine in the evening, dahlings.'

It goes without saying that these people are determined to create their own destiny. Sudden success has brought a new dimension to high society; scandals and scams are hot gossip, torrid love affairs with buddies of spouses are common, so are drawing room conversations on IPL betting, narcotics, high class escorts etc.

It goes without saying therefore that money is God in Delhi society and those who have it are much revered. So, possessing a Rolls Royce or a Ferrari is a status symbol and those who own three or more of these luxury cars have *arrived*.

With this comes the *Anything goes!* or *Sab chalta hai!* motto that the city has adopted; justify everything they have done or are willing to do, on the grounds that all is fair in the pursuit of their chosen destiny.

Delhi, the city that was built, destroyed and rebuilt several times, and has seen as many rulers, today stands a mute witness to this new kind of rulers who are determined to rewrite the city's history in their own way.

1

'Babes… Honey… *Jaan*… This is life calling. Is there anyone out there who has any zest left for me. Please pick up the phone and embrace me before you regrettably lose me.'

As I heard Reema's call go into the voice mail, I sped to my kitchen to answer it before she disconnected the line.

'Hey Reema, was in the shower, how are you doing? I just saw your message on Facebook last night, after work. Yes, work! Too much going on and I'm up against deadlines, trying to sell off some semi-abstract paintings before my next exhibition. I'm obscenely busy,' I said in one breath whilst catching it.

'Babes, no lame excuses! We haven't met for a whole decade and I don't care how absurdly abstract your life may become without selling your artwork because all I know is that I need to paint my life with new colours — silver to be precise. It's my 25th wedding anniversary and I need a few hen parties as I feel like I'm getting married all over again after all these centuries!'

Reema's voice was childlike as she shrieked through the phone in excitement. I had never heard anyone so ecstatic about celebrating their wedding anniversary, particularly after having lived with the same person for what would surely feel like hundreds of years. I could almost visualise her waltzing around the room, while she sang to me. She was insanely happy, as I was simply going insane with work.

'Babes, I've got the event company to bring in the Moulin Rouge show from Paris and a renowned singer is flying in from the US on the day. That's the surprise you are just gonna love and plenty of hash, booze and dishy men for you to choose,' said Reema breathlessly.

My ears were burning. Booze is normal, but hash? Moulin Rouge sounds extravagant and the singer from the US just sounds a bit over the top. I wasn't sure I was ready for such show of wealth... but I listened more than I spoke; only it was with a raised eyebrow.

Reema's tenacity could be likened to that of an athlete who is determined to win the race with all his might and muscle. This spirit has been evident in most aspects of her life; from making the grade in school to willfully getting married to someone who was now one of the most celebrated industrialists of India. She had always been an audacious and adamant personality, who knew how to get what she wanted and rarely what she needed. She was intensely ambitious and passionate about life. In recent times, I had only met Reema on Facebook or on BlackBerry Messenger. However, I was up to date with her life; her friends, her activities and her status that remained, married. I was in touch with her without feeling the need to meet her as life really had taken over with a vengeance. All the W's had overpowered me — work, worry, weight, water retention and wrinkles.

'But Reema. You've been married forever; 200 years to be precise. Why are you so excited about this love?' I asked, genuinely bemused.

'That's precisely why babes,' she chuckled. 'Most of my other close friends didn't make it to their 25th. It's a real cause for celebration nah and I believe I should get the lifetime achievement award or the Nobel Peace Prize to say the least. Just come babes. We'll have Tequila shots and dance the night away in the Aman Hotel before the big bash. There's a new nightclub there yah and it's fab. Come on babes, we'll hit on the hot men together while we down the shots and don't forget, 25 is the number. Twenty-five hen parties with 25 delicious men. Natasha, you and me. She's flying in too, and you haven't seen her forever either, *jaan*. You won't forget your trip for the next 25 years; I'll make sure that you have a rocking time. You deserve it babes. In fact we all do and I above all deserve a trophy in gold for having survived 25 years in this marriage of mine babes. It really is an achievement!' she laughed thunderously as she said this.

'I will do my best love. Let me sort out my over-demanding work schedule, my brooding business partner, my all-over-the-country hair, my unwaxed body and my ungroomed cat. In addition, I need to sort out my car which requires servicing; and that's pending for over a year, the dry cleaning that's quietly sitting in the corner of my bedroom for months and my unkempt apartment that I haven't vacuumed in weeks and not to forget the meals that have started moulding even in the refrigerator. You girls in Delhi don't need to worry your heads about any of these things. It is all laid out for you — from your food to your clothes to your men. I, on the other hand, worry about all that I have and much more about what I don't. And the one thing I do miss out here in London is not a man but a Man Friday who can cook, clean and wait on me all day long.'

Reema however was too excited about the forthcoming event of her life to give a thought to these mundane details of mundane existence.

'Natasha's going to let you know on Facebook, if she already hasn't, about her dates so that you can both co-ordinate, and it goes without saying *jaan* that you are both staying at my farmhouse. It's in DLF Chattarpur Farms, remember, and it's perfect for you guys. You will wake up to a clean and pristine landscape and could walk on the perfectly manicured lawns, barefoot. It would be so good for you. Afterwards, I'll get my maid Sarita to give you a wonderfully relaxing foot massage; I paid for her to learn reflexology. What's more babes I've trained my old servant Ramji to make wheatgrass juice every morning for me and my family. We all have a shot for glowing skin. You know I was so concerned about Varun's teenaged skin that was so full of acne but it's all vanished now, and Arun looks radiant too. As good-looking as their mother. You know we'll all walk barefoot — you, Natasha, the boys, Sandy and I, Ok? Babes! I gotta run. I have my laser appointment followed by an hour with my personal trainer and finally with my nutritionist. I need to go for my dress rehearsal too; Tarun needs me to be at his showroom by four as my personal stylist will be there. Catch you later babes. Love ya.'

Reema disconnected the call after the breathless five minute report on her life. She needed to take a crash course in the art of listening.

I had listened half attentively to Reema's propositions, as I didn't quite grasp why I would want to walk on the grass, barefoot, first thing in the morning. I brisk walked in Hyde Park every morning in my old shoddy trainers and I was certainly not lean, but definitely fit and healthy. Her paradoxical proposals of shots of the ominous wheatgrass in the morning and the even more ominous weed and Tequila shots in the night confused the living daylights out of me. I could not help but chuckle; perhaps there was more to Reema than what I had left behind 10 years ago. Her vivacious personality and her voracious appetite for more and more of absolutely everything always left me in wonder, but this was not a time for deep thoughts. What I needed to explore was my own willingness to fly back to what was once home but now sounded like an unexplored continent.

I was filled with nostalgia, thinking about our school days and how the three of us had been inseparable. We were all so different and yet shared the same space. The one commonality that stood out to me, at this moment, was our love for silly thrills and the ability to create them with spontaneity; the simple pleasure of having cold coffee at Depaul's in Janpath, with one eye on the hot guys on their motorbikes, could make our hearts beat faster than their bikes. We exchanged the most passionate glances with them but no numbers and still felt like we had eaten the forbidden fruit. This was almost a daily ritual until we grew up and turned a different corner.

I was not sure which corner I was going to turn in the next few days but Reema certainly did. It was either that she knew me better, than I did myself, or that she simply knew how to manoeuver people in her direction with all her charm, charisma and conviction.

No matter what I said regarding work commitments and the need to toil in these recession-ridden times, Reema was convinced that her anniversary should rank first on everyone's list of priorities. Reema was a go-getter whereas I just about managed to get-up-and-go to earn my bread by selling art, mostly by the top artists of India. My occupation was the only thing that added colour to my otherwise mundane days.

Reema had suggested that I travel light hence I packed my bags with minimum clothes, shoes and bags. But I was unable to offload the weight of all the memories that had given me so much of heartache as I left Delhi. Moving away to London had been easy, but had I really moved on, I now asked myself. Wasn't I dreading the coming days that would remind me of my distant past? Reema always laughed that she was the warrior while I had always been the worrier. Now I was worried about which memory would be triggered on this visit. Returning to my hometown after a decade or so could be testing the strength of my ability to make new beginnings; at least better than the ones I had managed to make previously.

2

I detest scales! That would be any and every kind whether it was for my body weight or for my travel luggage. They always show excess and that troubles me terribly. As much as I abhor getting my luggage weighed, I adore travelling. My choice of destinations ranges from practically anywhere in Europe to New York, California and Singapore, but now I was flying back to what had become a foreign territory.

From London Heathrow to Indira Gandhi International Airport, New Delhi takes approximately eight hours and 30 minutes on a Virgin Atlantic flight. It is not my preferred airline but then as long as it can adequately entertain me with the latest movies and a couple of palatable meals on premium economy, I'm not too bothered. I tend to look for reasonable comfort and value for money and I usually get it here. The stewards and hostesses are also accommodating and because I am a frequent flyer, I, at times, get upgraded.

It was 9:15 p.m. and I began to recline my seat before I ordered my customary cuppa. I glanced at the movie options and was happy to find two movies that I would be glad to engage in — *Bel Ami* and *Wanderlust*. I have a penchant for period films and I try not to miss any, and as for *Wanderlust*,

I am quite taken in by the movie, especially Jennifer Aniston; somehow I can relate to her girl-next-door look and down-to-earth attitude. I smile at my sense of accomplishment as I chalk out my activities for the next several hours on the flight. I even tick off my dinner. I feel a sense of satisfaction about choosing the right airline.

Before I risk sounding like I'm promoting Virgin Atlantic, I must let it be known why I am waffling on. See, although I'm a frequent flyer, I'm exceptionally nervous about travelling to Delhi for the first time in 10 years. It was after the turn of the century, year 2002, when I separated from my 13-year marriage in Delhi and willfully flew to London to build a life for myself; something in which I have eventually succeeded. Journalism took a back seat and art consultancy took over, as I needed to stay ahead of my mounting bills and the lifestyle I had chosen for myself. I had made a determination to not visit Delhi until my wounds were totally healed and my past had faded into insignificance — but then Facebook happened.

Reema convinced me to do something out of the box; that is to re-connect with our other classmate Natasha who has been globetrotting and had spent her last few months in Florence as a freelance writer before returning to New York. Her free-spirited nature made her travel to different continents engaging in various activities, besides writing and reporting, and we finally got in touch through Facebook. We were born and brought up in Delhi, where we spent all our college life together, and then parted ways when almost simultaneously I got married and her career transported her first to New York for two years, then Paris for another two. Then we lost touch for a while and I have no idea which corner she turned except I know she spends most of her time in New York.

Natasha is petite, pretty, polished and particularly mindful of her p's and q's. She has an impeccable dress sense as I know from the photographs she posts on Facebook; casual but smart during the days and elegant and sleek, with a touch of glamour, for the evenings when she is out partying. She relishes her wine and is probably a connoisseur, as even before she began her profession as a journalist, her parents had sent her to finishing school in Switzerland — it was common for parents in Delhi high society, in the '80s, to have their girls take such courses before they pushed them into marriages that finished them anyway. Natasha was way ahead of her times even in this; believing that a woman can truly remain complete without a man but she chose a series of them instead. She believed in dating a man until his wooing got dated. Every relationship seemed to be the *one* for her until the next one came along. Her attitude against a traditional backdrop, of Delhi, threw an all out challenge, but she dedicated herself to changing things around her in such a way that would allow her to make her own decisions. She confronted and challenged those who imposed their orthodox views on how a woman ought to lead her life.

Natasha fell in love with an American in New York back in the early '90s and was convinced that she had found the love of her life. He was a wild beast who she believed she could tame; a mistake most women make. He was a philanderer and even though he was untrustworthy she rode it out with him. In fact she was drawn to the exciting ride that he promised. Nobody knows when things changed and she decided that he may not be the one.

Life as I remember was never really simple in Delhi but then it was pretty straightforward. Modern School on Barakhamba Road kept both my social and love lives going as it had co-education, thankfully, and that kept my parents fairly broad-minded. This, in comparison to my cousins who had been raised in orthodox values, hence, were all married between the ages of 20 to 23 and had a couple of children; issues as some people in Delhi referred to them. As for me, I had other issues. I needed to prove my worth. I was an average student who went for a degree in English Honours in Lady Shree Ram College, worked as a freelance journalist for eight years while travelling and then tied the knot with my teenage sweetheart from school, at 30. He was the only one I knew, as I wasn't the kind to invite random men into my life. Life initially was smooth with many pleasant surprises but then came the shock and the wedding knot had to be loosened. The result: Now I don't pin my hopes on any man riding with me into the sunset.

Reema was an extrovert, I an introvert, whilst Natasha was an ambivert; somewhere between an intro and an extro. I dated the man I went on to finally marry so I very much believed in monogamy. Natasha on the other hand believed in gathering experiences. She always justified her flings as well as her initial failure in her career by stating that the more experience we have, the better it is for our personal development. She had a voracious appetite for dating and social media sites and was very proud to tweet about her latest date and then a few weeks later would report him as being dated. I do wonder what she learnt about men and life in all those years to have finally settled on sacred singlehood, where she gave herself the choice of living in different cities. She insisted that remaining single also gave her the option of having many male friends where each satisfied her differently.

Reema, as I remember, had the tendency to fall in love too quick, get hurt and then date another man on the rebound hoping that he would fix her broken heart as well as her fragmented life. The neglect by her parents, owing to the party scene that was on a dangerous overdrive in the late '80s, left her craving for attention. Her stupendous good looks beckoned her to become a model straight after high school; to walk the ramp, anywhere and everywhere in India, for some of the leading fashion designers in Delhi and Mumbai. By this time quite a few eminent names in the fashion industry hit Page 3. Reema too was featured regularly, first as a supermodel and then as a stunning socialite. There was no doubt that Reema made heads turn and male hearts churn at a single glance. Women, of course, envied her eternally slim waistline, oversized solitaires and limited edition designer handbags. Her heart was in the right place even though her mind had a tendency to flutter in diverse directions. She managed to find for herself the jewel in the crown when it came to marriage; a promising young man who was now a major industrialist — never mind the over-zealous pundit who found the match and profited immensely from the cash and gold from her parents; making sure it was the perfect horoscope match. When I left India she was a happily married woman and now she was busy planning her silver wedding anniversary.

As I adjusted my seat, sipped on my regular tea with sugar and merrily munched on my chocolate chip cookie, my mind travelled back to yesterday's call when Reema determined the packing of my suitcases with all the finer details.

'Babes, it's been a lifetime so I thought I should remind you of the things you might need. It's monsoon babes! Make sure you don't carry too much make-up as it is hot and humid. I'm sure you're still pretty with your voluptuous curves babes so do carry your sexy dresses as I need to hook you up. There are a few divorced men in our circle who are still fit with fat wallets. I don't even know what you look like since you never upload photos. I don't understand you. I even update my Facebook on the food I eat.' She had laughed heartily at this and added, 'Nowadays I'm essentially on green cuisine and raw eating; you know the very popular and trendy alkaline diet. I've loaded my farm with every possible herb and plants babes. You will become lean after my green cuisine and then I'll introduce you to a man who will nourish you in every possible way. Just come. I mean that literally and sexually.'

I laughed inwardly at her presumptuousness. I don't possess any so-called sexy dresses and neither am I possessed with the idea of getting hooked, as I prefer my meat to men which is much more orgasmic. Her green cuisine certainly wouldn't make me lean but make me mean and miserable instead, as I would be left hungry, hence angry. Being pencil-thin was never my goal in life. I was satisfactorily heavy and happy.

'Reema... but,' I had responded as *babes* was never my thing. I wanted to tell her that I was quite happy with my life.

Reema quickly intercepted.

'Babes you need to look hot. You are my friend and I'm going to introduce you to my circle of friends. It's my wedding anniversary; special one. We'll go clubbing 25 times. Sandy insisted that we go on a family cruise, with his parents tagging along, but I just wanted to celebrate in Delhi. Vick is back from his endlessly long business trip and he's dying to spend time with you and Natasha, even though you guys have been catching up in London. We are all going to be together again in dirty, but deliciously hot, Delhi where the temperature of the air and the men never goes down.'

She spoke endlessly, 'Babes, Delhi has changed. It's not the same place you left behind. It's become most desirable with fabulously fashionable bars, night clubs, cafés, restaurants and the most amazing high-end shopping mall which house all the high-end brands imaginable and is definitely my favourite destination. I get my latest handbags there that become my flavour of the month and I go for a new man every month, just to match it... Just kidding! I haven't reached the latter stage yet though some of my friends have. Delhi is brutally blazing with everything hot,' she said chuckling.

Twenty-five parties? Whatever! I smiled and frowned in the same breath as I thought of what I had left behind all those years ago and what I was about to encounter now. I had heard about the brutal decadence of the city and it was apparent that I would learn much about it during my visit.

Reema insisted that I acquire the taste of green tea to lose weight but I still continue relishing either my Earl Grey or English Breakfast.

I wondered now, as I took another sip of my sweet tea and switched on my TV screen, the real reason for destiny to invite me back to the city that both built my life and broke it in equal measure.

My history teacher at school once told us that the people and events around us are simply mirrors of who we are and that we must learn from them and not condemn or judge them — learn and move on, forgive and live, get and forget. Returning to Delhi was a test possibly of how much I had forgiven, forgotten and moved on, and if at all I had.

3

Time is an extraordinary thing — it changes pretty much everything from our inner landscapes to outer appearance to our geographical ones; the way we perceive things, to our attitudes and priorities, all change and alter with time. What had stood the test of time however was our friendship and no matter how our lives had changed, the emotions attached to this had remained somewhat constant.

I stepped into Delhi Airport Terminal 3 and it was most impressive and inspiring — a real contrast to the original one. The only thing that remained the same was the 'Welcome to Incredible India' billboard. It made me realise the timelessness of some things. I couldn't help but smile at the sight of it and of course I had no idea how incredibly Delhi had changed after I had bid it farewell almost a decade ago. I had heard and seen visuals of its changing hues on TV but then the spirit of a place never alters. Seema Kohli's art work was stretched across one wall whilst the distinguished artist, Paresh Maity's many panels were displayed across another; a real delight for the eyes.

After escaping the lecherous eyes of the immigration officer and his insistence on taking my mobile number,

I moved towards the conveyor belt only to be hounded by yet another over-zealous guy who was willing to unburden me by carrying my handbag and the suitcase that was about to arrive.

'Give Rs 500 and I take your bag to your car. You want taxi? I get you one... very cheap!'

I knew that was simply too much and I told him gently in Hindi that I wasn't a foreigner, so he shouldn't try to befool me and neither did I need a taxi. He insisted that this was the going rate and that it was non-negotiable. I had learnt to disregard such propositions during my life here. In fact, I had learnt to turn a deaf ear to plenty more nonsensical behaviour, such as eve-teasing and distasteful and derogatory remarks made by lewd men. Reema insists that she has never been subjected to such anti-social behaviour but that seems unrealistic in a city like Delhi where women of every age and social standing are subjected to this lecherous conduct.

A scrupulously clean C class black Mercedes was waiting outside the arrival lounge and Reema, with it, looked just as immaculate. Stunning in her stylish outfit, she invited quite a few second glances. She dashed towards me, flung her arms around me to lock me in her warm embrace for a few extended seconds, before she stepped back to inspect me.

'Look at you babes. Still as stunning as ever; my *Noor Jahan*. You haven't changed one inch besides gaining a few inches,' she teased. 'I'm going to put you on fresh vegetable juices and organic food as soon as we reach home. I'm going to detox you, botox you and get you out of your box. Babes, you'll drop a few kilos before you drop your pants; a few times on this trip I hope. I'm going to get you onto the hot looking men in this city who are as available as they are affluent. You are in for the ride of your life babes.'

'I'm the same old me.' I wasn't sure how well I took her observation but I simply smiled. What I did know for sure was that I didn't do organic. When hunger struck then anything edible did the trick. Having said that, I had been trying in vain to lose eight kilos for the past eight years but just hadn't got around to it and now I was lethargically working my way around my waistline. Seriously, weight had been my everyday battle and I was nowhere close to winning. Walking in Hyde Park could only shake off some negative thoughts from my mind but did nothing for my body and as far as men were concerned they were not a priority any longer either. I never craved for their attention or their accounts. Reema was keener to see my pants come down with a rich fellow than I had ever been. I was here for her and her celebration; nothing more.

We hurriedly sat in the car as parking immediately outside the exit was not permitted, except for Reema, of course, who always believed in bending the rules, if not breaking them. My luggage was carefully placed in the boot and Reema instructed the man wearing a crisp white cap, 'Driver Ramesh, please hurry. We are going to the farm.'

The chauffeur bowed his head obediently and in no time we were speeding away towards her home.

'Babes, we are all going to stay at the farm and I've informed Sandy. He has the choice to either stay with us, for these two weeks, or he can stay at the Westend residence with his nonchalant parents who don't care if they meet me or not in any case. The boys can come and go as they please. They have dozens of extra-curricular activities and Arun is learning golf with his dad every Sunday.' She was screeching in excitement, and added, 'You know babes, Varun is learning the guitar as well as kick boxing and karate. In addition, he has his own band with a couple of school friends. He is incredibly handsome and yet so innocent; my Varun. He's all of 17, but so mature and masculine. He's studying for his SAT too babes as he wants to go either to USC or NYU next year. His cousins also study there so it's easier. Anyway babes I'm soooo excited that you're here. We are all going to have a blast! We will rock the city! There is just too much to catch up on.'

'Of course, that's why I'm here, to catch up on lost time and add more magnificent memories. So tell me, when exactly does the fun begin?' I said trying to muster the same amount of enthusiasm.

'Tonight!' screamed Reema. 'We'll go to B Bar. It's a new club that has been opened by my very close friends. We'll down a few shots and head for the airport around one in the morning to pick up Natasha. While we party the driver will go and have his dinner. I'll give him a little extra besides what he gets as overtime. He's cool.'

As Reema blabbered on, I looked out of the car window, at the city that I had left behind so many years ago, trying to see if I could spot any changes. There is one thing about being in a car that I can't seem to change; that is to start daydreaming. I've been engaging in this since childhood and my reverie begins by gazing up at the clouds. I imagine walking on them and while doing so my mind wanders off to many far off places. Now as I gazed up I realised that the dark clouds were threatening rain; there was no escaping it. The air was misty and almost magical as it stirred certain emotions in me. I loved the dewy, damp air that somehow never dampened my spirits, like it did with others. I wondered, however, if staying at Reema's farm was after all a good idea, as the lawns would become mucky with the rain; not to mention the threat of mosquito-borne diseases like dengue and malaria. I had carried my repellent and was increasingly glad to have done so now that she had made our arrangements at her farm.

Reema was a planner and I dare not intervene in her regimented programmes. Ever since I can remember, she has always been the organiser and a very good one at that, while Natasha and I have blindly followed instructions. That saved us the hassle of expending our energy on putting things together and it also saved us from getting into conflicts with each other. We understood each other's strengths and weaknesses and respected them.

I sensed a sea change in the new landscape of Delhi; its vibe was different and I wondered now how enriched and how impoverished it had become through the ferocious winds of change.

I also wondered how much Reema had changed over these years; how much of her personality — her effusive welcome — was real against the backdrop of the ever-changing city of Delhi and its decadent character.

4

Delhi is a city of sharp contrasts — there are those who live in the abominable depths of despair and abject poverty and then there are those who live with abundant wealth that afforded them an obscenely opulent lifestyle. The contrast could not be sharper. My eyes travelled from the clouds to the ground where the landscape of the people, who lived on the other side, was still as appalling as it had been when I left Delhi many years ago.

As we drove on, I took in the other sights and sounds of the city. Driving down Vasant Kunj we passed a couple of plush malls, posh schools offering international standard education and newly built hospitals believed to possess the latest medical equipment, on the left side, and small, humble stores, on the right, that were practically dilapidated but still generated an income for the people who tried to compete with the city's fast changing face of retail business. We passed some tall trees that stood majestically in one neat row. Delhi was green, but far from clean, as litter was strewn all over. There was exquisite beauty and extreme ugliness all rolled in one and I felt love and hate for all that I observed around me.

Reema was on her mobile making a re
tonight and after hanging up she began texting someo
brought a sudden glow on her pretty and perfectly sculpted
face. She seemed oblivious to her surroundings; as if she had
created a world all of her own that kept her insulated.

'It's my son,' Reema announced as if sensing my curiosity.
She showed me the text which read, '*Sup, in Nick's farm. See
y sn. lmao*'. 'He always does this and I simply love it. He
sends me messages all day long. This keeps me well informed
about his whereabouts. He is just so transparent babes; I'm
so blessed. You know my friend Shalini, her son is the same
age as mine, but he already bets in the IPL cricket matches
and smokes pot all day. The kid's lost it, as have many others
in our friends' circle. They burn the money that their fathers
unrelentingly earn. But my Varun is a simple boy. He would
never gamble or get into drugs. He is so responsible and so
admirably attached to me babes as I am to him. Let me just
respond to my baby,' she said with a smile.

'Sure love. You must,' I responded as she swiftly pressed a
few keys and then turned her head towards me with a broad
smile and a gleam in her big brown eyes.

She was clearly very pleased that I had made the effort to
come over to celebrate her big day. She hadn't changed much,
not outwardly at least; in fact she looked even happier than
she did back then… and younger. Her marriage was clearly
rendering her the contentment that every woman sought.

We drove past the most magnificent Chattarpur
temple with its white marble facade and intricate carvings.

Its vastness was awe-inspiring. It was also home to many foreigners who stayed in the ashram for meditation and prayer; on the road to self-discovery. They had realised that life was worth more than the size and scale of one's possessions and perpetual ambitions.

Before we knew it we had arrived at Reema's palatial farm. I had been here before, but clearly the memories of its plush beauty had not been locked in my mind; it was as though I was visiting the place for the first time. I took in the elegant surroundings. In the centre of the verdant open lawns was a fountain with a 20 feet high Buddha, carved out of black stone, sitting serenely beside it. The exquisiteness of the surroundings superseded any resort that I had ever lodged in. As the car halted, Reema gave some instructions to her driver, for the night. My door was opened for me by one of her retinue of servants in starched, white uniforms. As I stepped out, I took a deep breath and thanked the servant with a broad smile while he silently bowed his head.

I noticed that a glow had settled on Reema's face as she enthusiastically heralded me into her earthy and ethnic home that she had designed herself with a touch of Sandy's inputs. Her smile broadened as she excitedly motioned me into what was to be my room that was simply huge with minimalistic yet rich furnishings, with its own attached glass bathroom with a rain shower and jacuzzi. The view of the gardens was panoramic and the only thing that would shield me were abundant plants situated outside the translucent glass wall.

Breathtaking!

'I love it Reema. This is divine.' I could not help expressing my wonder.

'It's a-w-e-s-o-m-e right? Babes you being here is just awesome and I can't believe I'm seeing you after all these years. I'm going to make you lose weight in these two weeks and your skin will glow by the time you return to London. I'm going to introduce you to a new lifestyle and a new man that you can carry back with you. You are going to substitute food with saucy men who will make you thin; thin is in. Just think of positive shrinking babes,' she said while breaking into a thunderous laughter. She then rang the bell and immediately a man in a crisp white safari suit arrived. He was five feet four inches tall, bald and very slim with a serene smile. She instructed him to get us the freshly prepared vegetable juice followed by organic green vegetables — delightful and delicious according to her and depressing and distasteful according to me.

His name was Shamji, I later learnt, and he had been with Reema and Sandy for the past 12 years. Now that Reema had become a health freak, she had trained him, along with all her other servants, on the art of organic living.

I excused myself after forcefully consuming the odious green and lean cuisine, as I needed my nap. Besides, having lived in London for almost a decade I had got used to plenty of private time and that strictly meant that no one was permitted to cross these boundaries. The travel and the apprehension and excitement of this visit were finally taking its toll on me. I desperately needed a nap. Reema looked sufficiently pleased at my decision as she had things to do. She pressed some keys on her BlackBerry and then at the speed of lightening whizzed out of my room and into her BMW, leaving the Mercedes behind in case I needed to step out on my own.

I lay on the well-kept bed in my opulent room and as I closed my eyes I felt a pang of angst in my chest. The city that had given me both abundant love and ample pain had beckoned me to return and I earnestly wondered why. I told myself to let go of the past and focus on the present — I visualised Reema, Natasha and myself sitting on a beach in Goa with exotic cocktails in our hands and a radiant warm glow on our faces.

Happiness had found a place in our hearts and we had all arrived at a place of real ease with ourselves. It's generally the case with women in their forties. We no longer needed to prove our worth as we had learned to love and accept ourselves along the way and outside opinion had very little to do with how we viewed ourselves. The experiences of life taught us to finally be comfortable in our own skins as nothing else really mattered; the superficialities transcended and broken hearts mended. In the final analysis I had learnt to truly love myself for a man to love me but then did I want a man in my life at this point; that was the real question. If I visualised a man beside me right now then I may just get him and that could be a scary space to be in. It was the laws of attraction thing.

With a hundred and ten thoughts floating in my head I finally began to feel drained and depleted. Just as I was about to nod off there was an enthusiastic knock on my door, and before I could utter a word in my stupor, a medium height, fair and comely man entered my room.

'Hey Zoya! Welcome to India! So good to have you here. Long time babes; wow, you sure are a babe.'

Before I knew it Sandy's arms were around me as he enveloped me into a bear hug. I could feel his biceps as he sealed me snugly in his embrace. Welcoming me to his home he walked around checking whether I had everything I needed. He then called in Shamji and instructed him to take special care of me.

'Zoya, you are my royal guest. I just had to meet you after my golf. I teed off at 5 a.m. as its Saturday and I played nine holes. I'm staying in Westend with my parents and the boys. Reema will be here with you throughout your stay. You gorgeous ladies have fun and if you need anything you can call me on my number. Just note it down. Now let me quickly show you my new library while we have some fresh fruit juice. I'm sure Reema must've already forced her repulsive green vegetable juice down your throat.' We both chuckled, as he obviously knew his wife well.

He took me by the hand and walked me to a white room with long bookshelves lined across two walls on either side. There were family photographs — all framed in a single style on one of them; many captured in Verbier during their skiing holidays and a few exotic cruises, and on the other, were impressively lined Sandy's photographs with many politicians, actors and foreign diplomats. There was one in which he was shaking hands with Barack Obama and in another with Margaret Thatcher in the '80s. Then in the far corner I noticed one with Reema and him with Bill Clinton, having dinner at the Bukhara restaurant at the Sheraton Hotel. They both looked really happy in each one of them. In today's world, where love was precarious and far from predictable, they were lucky to have each other.

On a wall in the room hung diplomas and certificates whilst below sat the many trophies he had won in his golf tournaments. I quietly wondered if he was good enough for the Ryder Cup. I smiled as I congratulated him on his accomplishments; the biggest one being his very successful marriage. He just shrugged and smiled.

Above his green antique Chesterfield chair there was a collection of art works by Satish Gujral and M.F. Hussain and on the narrow wall beside the window hung Ram Kumar's landscape. In fact, each wall had a painting or a photograph by the most eminent artists of India. I finally feasted my eyes on my all time favourite photographer's magnum pictures. Sandy noticed and he proudly said that he knew Raghu Rai well and would introduce me to him during my two-week stay. 'I'll invite him and his stunning wife to our anniversary bash. That's if he's not busy visiting the ashram that he frequents.'

Sandy continued and I could detect the pride in his voice, 'You know Zoya, I'm a self-made man who has earned it all through perspiration, perseverance and practical decisions; nothing of what Indians ordinarily believe to be luck or blessings of an unseen one who sits up there and waves a magic wand for us to have it all. I am the creator of my own destiny and I believe I've done a splendid job.'

As his royal guest I didn't want to counter his claim so I simply commended him for his achievements. Besides, his achievements were far from ordinary and most praiseworthy, so I applauded him without bringing God into it.

The room was probably worth millions and Sandy was like a little boy eager to flaunt his many trophies. The sparkle in his eyes was a reflection of his pride and joy. I was sure Reema was equally proud of his many accomplishments.

Just then Shamji knocked on the door with a glass of freshly squeezed orange and pomegranate juice for both of us. I drank it even though I was sufficiently full. Where in God's name would I squeeze fresh juice for myself in London? But I savoured the taste. It really was more palatable than the repulsive vegetable juice.

There is nothing in the world that can possibly beat the Indian hospitality. I thanked Sandy for the tour and the juice as he left to have his morning tea and read his newspapers by the pool at the rear of the farm. He asked me if I would like to join him but I politely turned down the offer, as I seriously needed to rest before heading out again in the night. I asked him if he would be joining us to which he replied, 'I'm busy tonight with some foreign delegation. Boring stuff but someone has to do it. You girls enjoy yourselves and we'll catch up soon, but if there's anything you need, please don't hesitate to call.'

Sandy had always been the man of Reema's dreams and I could clearly see why. A good marriage was a rare jewel nowadays and it was a delight to know that they were so happy with each other. It was obvious that they even looked after themselves to always remain attractive for each other. He obviously worked out and not a hint of age showed on him. In fact even though they were exactly the same age as I, they were both 20 years younger than me in spirit. They complemented each other beautifully.

I watched him stroll outside from my window after he gave me a quick peck on the cheek and after a quick click of the fingers that summoned his personal valet.

I realised how much I had missed the Indian way of life and the warm-heartedness of the people; after all Indians believed that receiving guests in their homes was like receiving God.

I knew, without a speck of doubt, that I was going to be treated no less than a Goddess in these two weeks.

5

I felt as fresh as the flowers that bloomed in Reema's lush garden, when I finally woke up. Cheerful voices outside had woken me up and before I went out to greet who it was outside, I dashed into the rain shower to revive myself.

Varun, Arun and Reema were sitting by the poolside picking on fresh fruit and nuts. As I walked towards them the boys stood up to greet me. Reema was texting. Varun surely was handsome, 17 years of age, fit and almost six feet tall, and Arun was cute and fat. He was all of 11 and so he had layers of puppy fat while I sensed layers of attitude in Varun. I simply smiled as he pushed forward his knuckle and said, 'Yo!'

I'm never quite sure how to respond to this generation's gestures, so I am most comfortable being my conservative self that ordinarily responds with the good old-fashioned 'Hello' and 'How do you do?' as 18th century as it may sound, but then, I admittedly was from another century. I know no better just as he probably knows no better either. It's the new-age lingo that's cool.

Sitting beside Arun was the comeliest and cutest pug I had ever set my eyes on. He stared at me and wagged his tail in anticipation of me kneeling down and stroking him, which I did. He was affectionate as he was affable. We became buddies in no time.

'His name is Cleo and he's four-years-old. He stays with me as I am his favourite,' boasted Arun.

Varun was quick to interject in a more serious tone, 'He's with you buddy cause I'm busy with stuff. He was my 13th birthday present, remember. Anyway. He is sick man.'

If I didn't know better I would have believed Cleo to be sick, as in ailing, but my nephews and nieces kept me updated on some of the new age dialect that translated sick as excellent or awesome. They believed every new gadget or gimmick to be sick and even their pop and movie idols were nothing less than sick. The poor guys! Some of them looked seriously sick and anemic anyway.

Arun remained reluctantly quiet and it was clear to see that he didn't want to mess with his big brother or with his still bigger ego. He bent down towards Cleo and began playing with him. Cleo was well-groomed and wore a crimson Paul Smith collar around his furry neck. I was told that his favourite one though was Dolce & Gabbana.

Reema mildly intervened by stating that everyone loved Cleo and he loved everyone equally. She insisted that he belonged to everyone while she continued to press the keys on her mobile, texting continuously.

That was the most insipid response to the situation but I guess it worked as Varun threw an apple across the lawns for Cleo to chase and for Arun to run swiftly after him. The air was clear and crisp at this time of the day and the sky was a pale blue with a few floating clouds that may annoy us with rain later in the day.

Reema was still texting someone very swiftly on her BlackBerry and she intermittently looked up to make small talk with me. She evidently shared a very intimate relationship with her mobile.

She munched on a few black grapes and then some pomegranate seeds before she spoke. 'Babes, a few of my friends are also joining us tonight. You will absolutely love them. You may remember Himani from our school. She was a batch senior. I reconnected with her since she has really come up in the world. From a miss nobody she is now one of the wealthiest women in the city. She moves around in a Rolls Royce and her husband owns a Bentley and an Aston Martin. Her kids study at the Step by Step International School in Noida and they travel in their Porsche Cayenne. They live on Prithviraj Road and they throw the most obscenely ostentatious bashes in the city. They are so flashy and flamboyant and they rock.'

'Himani? I kind of remember her. Tall, slim but not so good-looking, if I may say so, but she was a brain and remained somewhat aloof; not very friendly at all. No style but plenty of substance,' I recalled.

'That's the one. But now babes she's hot stuff as she's had work done on herself; face and body sculpting. Now she's a babe with style and substance and recently while her husband was away on his business trip she met an expatriate. She's all over him; getting laid each time her better half goes away, which seems quite often. Anyway please don't let on; I mean she confided in me and doesn't want anyone to spill the beans. We all need to defend our territory, you know what I mean? Her husband being filthy rich she's having her cake and eating it too. Bless her! She is great fun to be with and the men obviously think so too. She is a very practical woman and a real diva,' said Reema, filling me on all the details of Himani's life.

'Whatever makes her happy,' was my lukewarm response. 'By the way, Sandy showed me around his library. It's really fab. He was like a schoolboy boasting his many accomplishments. It was sweet of him to take out time for me.'

'Ahhhh! His room that displays his over-sized ego. Whatever! Anyway, we are all meeting for dinner at the Emporio Mall first and then we are going clubbing. Okay? So the look is sexy and smart with a designer handbag. Prada is great but Birkin is better,' she said with a tinkling laugh.

Who hadn't heard of the ultra luxurious Emporio Mall that housed practically all the leading high-end brands of the world? I think people in the remotest parts of the world knew about the Emporio Mall in Delhi. Everyone ranted and raved about its grandeur and I was about to set foot in it for the very first time and was sure it would be an eye-opener and a wallet-opener as well.

Reema was still texting with a tender expression on her face and I wondered who she was sending messages to, since her sons were right here at the farm although they were no longer visible. I asked her where they had disappeared.

'Oh, in the snooker room babes. Varun is teaching the little one how to play on our new Philippe Starck table. You know babes, Varun appears angry and hassled all the time but really he's a great kid. He just has so much pressure with it being his final year at the British School and then the strain of SAT and making the grade to gain acceptance in one of the top universities in the US.'

Reema had obviously picked up on my silent disapproval of Varun; his abundant self-confidence bordering on haughtiness was certainly not appreciated by me. My own brother's children in London were in the same age bracket as Varun, but their verbal and body language were definitely more affable. They most certainly did not have an attitude like Varun's. They were more down to earth.

Reema continued, 'England is not even an option babes, as America is more vast in every sense. The UK is small and conservative and you know our kids have grown up with the American influence. The States is home and Varun's aunt resides in a pretty villa in Vegas which is just a stone throw away from L.A.'

'So true,' I agreed. 'America and its culture is idolised here. The American fast food chains and multinational companies have found a ground here in the Indian society. Even their accent has found a place on the tongues of many Indians, some of who have never even stepped on American soil,' I mocked, and added, 'They are known as the Amerindians.'

Reema laughed but rather than responding to this mockery continued texting or BBM-ing or whatever.

I knew I had to get accustomed to it. It was clearly an addiction for her.

'Can I have tea as I need my cuppa in the morning,' I asked, attempting to elicit a response from her. 'I don't mind the traditional milky *masala* tea either if it's possible. Honey is preferable to sugar and perhaps an oatmeal or digestive biscuit too if there is one.'

Reema immediately stopped texting and frowned upon the idea as if I had asked her for drugs. 'Are you crazy?'

She suggested that I have hot water instead or at the most a mild herbal tea without any biscuits. Then she insisted that since it was almost lunchtime, I could have a fresh mint tea with leaves that also grew in her garden, right after my meal. I wondered if there was any plant or herb that grew here which we weren't going to consume.

She had more advice to give on the advantages of a healthy body. 'I did my yoga early morning with my yoga and meditation instructor and later I'll go for my Pilates class. You ought to accompany me babes. My gym is in a plush mall and you can stroll around and subsequently join me there where you can sit in the juice bar and feast your eyes on the panoramic view outside. When you get tired of that you can feast your eyes on the hot men and their perfectly sculpted bodies. They are half our age and unbelievably fit; they're awesome babes and there are so many of them. Each one is hotter than the other and is most likely available. Just let me know which one you want and I will immediately introduce you to him. I know them ALL.'

It sounded like a plan. I hadn't feasted my eyes on dishy men for a very long time as work had completely taken over my life. However, for me, they were good from far and far from good. I had already been bitten and I certainly wasn't interested in being smitten anymore. I was quite convinced that I was now living happily ever after without a man.

'I'm reading John Grisham right now so I'll carry it with me. It's almost over so if there's a bookstore there I'll pick up any other bestseller. You don't have to bother about me,' I clarified.

'Sure babes, and once I'm done, I'll sit with you in the juice bar and while sipping a wheatgrass drink, fill you in on who's wife is making out with who's husband. Some of these women prefer the hot personal trainers while most settle for the friends of their respective husbands. Most of them come to the gym to get fit and fixed.'

'So, they are taking care of their hearts, practically and metaphorically.' I could not keep myself from commenting sarcastically.

Reema laughed and continued, 'The age management business is thriving in this city since people are eager to look their best for their lovers. You may notice that some of them appear younger today than they did 10 years ago, owing to their botox and beau. And the 'flavour of the month' is quick to change. They get tired of each other after a while. I guess it's really all about the chase. Women here have finally learnt to be practical by putting their emotions aside.'

She finally placed her mobile down and looked up at me with a contented smile. 'You know most wives are as fit as a fiddle and the husbands are fit enough to be fiddled with.'

We both broke into a giggle.

She looked radiant with her hair up in an unkempt ponytail; Nike sports T-shirt and track pants revealed her slim silhouette. She was definitely fit enough to be fiddled with, I observed; with all the right contours. But in my heart I was quite confident that her loyalty lay only with Sandy; the love of her life.

6

The restaurant was heaving and as we entered, the comely manager approached Reema with utmost courtesy.

'Ma'am, your table is ready and some of your guests are already here. Would you like to go ahead with your meal or would you care to have a drink at the bar?'

Reema was already heading for the bar towards a fine-looking young guy in his thirties. After a few air kisses she introduced me as her friend from London. I watched as she flirted with him, touching his toned biceps almost lovingly and laughing uproariously at some remark. In the din of the music and the voices around me, I could not really catch their conversation. After a while, she placed her well-toned arm through mine and walked us to our table.

The restaurant had a pleasing ambience; dim lights and enough of open space. It was busy but thankfully not noisy. It offered every cuisine under the sun and looking at the menu I realised that I was famished.

Reema introduced me to her friends who, I noticed, were all stunning; fit, with not an ounce of flab on them. I wondered how I would eat in front of all these figure conscious women.

The evening however turned out to be easy as I did remember Himani and a couple of other friends from the yesteryears so the conversation had a ring of familiarity to it. As the evening wore on, I began observing this mix of high society women. One of them had the poise and grace of Audrey Hepburn and said little; Anishka wore her confidence like a talisman and obviously didn't need youth-enhancers like botox and other cosmetic procedures. It was not her lack of lines but her confidence that was the secret of her beauty; she was articulate and exuded intelligence. A few of the others were eager to dress up their life stories in order to impress but I took that in my stride. In fact, I found their made-up tales and their gossip about their absentee so-called friends, rather amusing.

'You know girls Priyanka was caught making out with her husband's right hand man. They were caught in the act,' said one of them.

To this somebody responded, 'Better than Manisha who sleeps with this hideous looking politician who gets her husband licenses for various dealerships. Apparently her husband encourages her to sleep with influential men for his personal gain.'

I was introduced to more stories about the happenings of Delhi high-society.

I had never seen so many Louis Vuitton, Hermés and Gucci bags together in one room and it seemed like the stores themselves had walked into the restaurant where Reema and her friends wined, dined and whined.

The evening wore on...

Name-dropping, ultra-luxurious holiday destinations and resorts and the latest high-end brands were an intrinsic part of the conversations as were the flashy cars and clubs that were part of their lives. The colourful conversations did not end there; they rolled with laughter as each undressed their personal trainers with saucy words.

Said one, 'Man! Mine is as hot as the chicken *tikka* cooking on your hot barbeque counter. His ass is as firm as his biceps and it's only him I fantasise about when having to make out with my husband. But someday, I won't need to fantasise anymore; I'll have the real thing. I'm just building a rapport with him. The last time I went he was staring at my cleavage. The boob job was worth it.'

Divya, another friend of Reema's, revealed how she left home in her track pants, asking her driver to take her to the gym where she met her lover; the husband of an acquaintance, who she joked was an MBA — married but available — who then drove her to a hotel room that she paid for. Plenty of people she knew ended up booking rooms with their respective partners in the same hotel. Later she returned to the gym where the driver would be waiting. I mused that this was the daily workout that kept her slim and smiling in equal proportions. And men believed that polygamy was only their territory.

They finally went on to whine about their husbands and their in-laws as they sipped on their exotic cocktails and gave a glad eye to any desirable man who walked by.

Even as they chatted I watched their animated faces. With their tiny waists and huge designer bags they were as different as they were similar; some were working, while others were sitting at home but investing in the share market. They exchanged notes on the price of gold and other stocks. Sonakshi, for instance, announced, without regret, that she had lost to the tune of 20 lakhs in her latest investments. I noted that these women were confident in their own skins and living a hedonistic life out of choice.

But there were also exceptions...

There was one woman who was even wealthier than Reema and didn't feel the need to dirty her hands (as Reema had described) by working or investing, except on her eternal youth. According to Reema, she flew to L.A. regularly to get herself fixed and her very recent acquisition was her pouting lips. Her big rocks and her bigger Hermés handbag spoke about her bulky bank balance. As Reema explained on an aside, 'She's big babe and she's driven in in a Bentley Continental Coupe while her husband just bought the new Continental GT V8 to park next to his red Ferrari F12 Berlinetta, his yellow Lamborghini Aventador and a C class Mercedes, for everyday use. Her kids are both studying in the US and she is a globetrotter who travels only first class and hires her own chauffeur wherever she goes. What more can a woman ask for babe? It's another story that her husband has been behind bars a few times for this and that, but she remains in her comfortable territory. He too has become bolder after his stints in jail. In fact, he feels he's become invincible.'

While chatting, the subject turned to Reema's anniversary bash and they all boasted how much they would spend on their designer apparel and the matching accessories. I learnt that these women never bought things on sale. Because of their frequent international trips they knew what was hot, and if they were not waiting for the style to arrive in India, they were making trips to Paris and Milan for exclusive ensembles.

Reema insisted that they come dressed like never before, as top industrialists, distinguished politicians and top Bollywood stars would be attending the party. Sandy would be spending an obscene amount on security even though each eminent personality would be accompanied by their own bouncers. She then added that she didn't expect gifts, but would prefer if they donated to her private NGO; she wanted cheques so that the media could click photographs of her and her friends posing with them.

I mutely listened and ate my meal as the only unfashionably overweight individual who shamelessly polished her spicy Thai chicken curry with rice while being entertained with their spicier stories. The rest ordered salads or sushi and by the end of the meal even their lipsticks did not get smudged since they chatted more than they chewed. Reema had whispered to me earlier that most of them were on the alkaline diet and she hoped that I too would get roped into it. I passed her a quick glance of disapproval and tucked my hand into the breadbasket.

At precisely 10:30 p.m. Reema called for the bill and after it had been cleared she sprang up from her chair to take a call in private. I could not help giving her a curious stare as she walked towards the exit, while chatting with the caller in a hushed, almost inaudible, tone as we all followed her out. The women air kissed each other goodnight and headed in different directions.

Reema hastily instructed her driver to head towards B Bar in Saket. She looked rather tense and was fidgety but I refrained from probing and instead chose to calmly go with the flow.

There was a lot of traffic on the road.

The infrastructure had developed tremendously in the recent years, with many flyovers built for the purpose of easing up the traffic that had surely swollen. Reema told me that the city of Delhi had been struck with incurable insomnia; that accounted for the number of cars on the road and even pedestrians. Street vendors were still busy even at this time of the night. During my time there were only hotels to dine in, at this late hour. Late nights usually were for the night shows and the Chanakya Cinema was our usual haunt for the weekly movie.

As we entered the bar, Reema's eyes seemed to be searching for someone and within seconds a young, good looking man, in his early thirties, sprinted towards us and extended his hand out at me as Reema introduced us. His sweeping glance at me may have been most unflattering but the manner in which his gaze locked with Reema could not be described as anything but amorous. I sensed a spark between them but quickly dismissed the thought as being a product of my overactive imagination or too many glasses of cocktail earlier.

Just as I was looked around, taking in the ambience of the place, I couldn't help but notice this young man's hands travelling to Reema's waist and gradually down to her hips and then finding residence there. Now it was more than his gaze that was locked to Reema's; his chest moved closer to her bosom and she appeared delighted. They were as intimate as they could possibly get with their clothes on. He wriggled his hips into hers, as they were oblivious to the world around them.

I took a deep breath, as I wanted to call out to him to intercept him in case his hands decided to travel to other parts of her anatomy. Of course I forgot his name, as is usually the case with me, 10 seconds after being introduced to someone. I would never make a good PR person, I thought, but this time I could be excused as there were plenty of thoughts floating through my head at this very awkward moment.

Reema seemed to have become aware of the fact that my eyes were travelling faster than his hand, so she unlocked herself swiftly to be with me in no time, giggling away like a mischievous teenager.

'Babes, Amit is everything to me.' She sounded excited and continued, 'He is like a life coach. He trains with me in the gym, does the salsa with me and we regularly attend the landmark classes together. He is so intelligent babes and he teaches me the Art of Living; advises me on every aspect of my life. He lifts me when I am down. He really perks me up baby.' And after a few seconds, she added, 'Isn't he c-u-t-e? I mean check out his butt.'

I couldn't help feeling that there was more to it given their body language and the kind of vocabulary they used with each other; it suggested a kind of intimacy that could not be overlooked, no matter how Reema tried to dress it up. It was kind of strange given her near-perfect relationship with her husband Sandy.

We had a few drinks together and immersed ourselves in chatter and laughter and I noticed Reema and Amit exchange passionate glances. Amit looked in my direction too during the conversation but it was apparent that he was smitten by her. He listened to her in rapt attention as she spoke gregariously. I felt like a *kebab mein*... basically an unwanted guest.

'Babes isn't this place rocking?' Reema asked me. 'I just l-o-v-e coming here. How about you *jaan*?' She asked Amit, swaying to Usher and then to Lady Gaga. '*Jaan*! We must dance tonight! By the way babes, that's the surprise... Lady Gaga! We are flying her over for the big night. Isn't that great? The DJ will have us all falling in love again.' She said excitedly while gazing into Amit's amorous eyes. 'I wanted Usher to come. I just l-o-v-e the way he makes me swing my hips. Amit, you like the way I move nah baby?'

'*Jaan*! Right now I want you to move to my tune,' he said seductively while gazing into her eyes and pulling her towards him. 'I'm the one who'll tell you how to swing your hips, Ok baby?'

Lady Gaga? Nice. But isn't that a tad too extravagant?

Reema and Amit were making me very uncomfortable now. I could accept the *Jaan* as Delhi lingo, but they were practically undressing each other with their eyes.

While Amit went away to order more drinks a few friends came over to greet us. I was meeting them after years. I noticed one of the guys staring at Reema with starving eyes, evidently longing to do it with her. She chatted casually with him definitely aware of what was on his mind. She probably found it flattering.

Reema and I finally got the opportunity to catch up on our lives. We had been the best of friends as we grew up but now I felt that I was getting acquainted with her all over again. Certain traits in people remain constant over the years, and in Reema I could see that her determination had remained intact. However our experiences force us to mould ourselves; Reema too had changed into this social butterfly. She had always been outgoing but now there was a certain brazenness in the way she interacted with the world around her.

This is not the night for this kind of analysis, I checked myself. It was time to relive and revive our friendship.

Our conversation was disrupted only when Amit placed our drinks before us. He told us of a near brawl at the bar, which explained why it took him this long to get the drinks. Apparently the son of some political bigwig was enraged at not being served on time. The loud music drowned his obscenities but those around the bar heard him screaming his lungs out. He had made quite a spectacle of himself till he was given attention. He was accompanied by a motley crowd; some Indian men and Russian and Czech girls.

I recognised that such behaviour was nothing but the consequence of an ego trip; favourable fortune lead to power and that in turn gave rise to the need to control and manipulate. However, at times the reason was diametrically the opposite — the waylaid ministers raised wayward children; Delhi's bratpack who felt they were above the law. In either case the outburst stemmed from insecurity and low self-esteem, hence the almost desperate need to prove their worth by being brash and bullying. I wondered, however, if this extreme ego had become endemic to Delhi society — the attitude of *I have money hence the power to buy absolutely anything and anyone anytime and when I do, so what...* Anything goes, doesn't it?'

Though the music was deafening, the shrieks of certain people could still be heard only because they wanted to be heard. Empty vessels make the most sound I thought. People can be likened to music; some speak to touch others hearts while others are sheer noise. Some loved to draw attention — they needed the recognition, and others genuinely couldn't hear each other speak so they yelled.

Reema just chuckled on my raising an eyebrow, as if she was accustomed to this kind of abominable display of ego and abrasive behaviour. Now that Amit was back at the table, she had eyes only for him as she sipped on her Margarita provocatively, as if the glass were his lips. I tried to determine how those around her saw her; she was stunning in her skin-tight gold dress that showed just the right amount of cleavage and her long thick chestnut hair had been blow dried to perfection. She had a unique alluring quality that made people gravitate towards her. Her laughter was contagious and each time she laughed flashing her perfectly set pearlies, her entire face lit up like a 100-watt bulb. All night long she wore a beatific expression that made her appear even more beautiful.

We had a memorable night with moments when my eyes opened wide in stunned surprise. A guy I knew from the bygone days, who was happily married then, was now seen flirting with another woman in her twenties. Another acquaintance in her forties was chatting away, in rather intimate terms, with a guy in his early thirties who was endowed with a perfectly chiselled body. His perfectly chiselled hand did not budge all night from her near-perfect ass and ample bosom that almost spilled out of her skin-hugging dress.

What scandalised me the most were teenage boys and girls partying there with a similar agenda; of who's picking up whom. Reema was clearly familiar with this kind of display while I likened it to the Jackie Collins books I read while growing up — *Hollywood Wives*, its supposed sequel, *Hollywood Husbands* and later, *Hollywood Divorces*. Reema had been right in saying that everything American had found its way into Delhi. I chuckled as I thought that these high society gatherings could be best described under the title, *Delhi Wives, Delhi Husbands and Delhi Divorces*. I guess I had to take this sort of behaviour in my stride, as it was part and parcel of the new India — the India that was perhaps fast becoming as incredulous as it was incredible; as flawed as it was fabulous.

Reema had followed my gaze and laughing aloud said, 'She's drop-dead gorgeous babes, who would drop everything for a man who is loaded; in his pants and in his pocket. I know Megha so well. She is a politician's daughter and men find her hot even though she is an easy catch. Her over-the-top wedding celebration lasted 10 days and her marriage 30! Her man already had a Russian beauty on the side and now he lives with her. After that she let her hair down and everything else, as life had let her down. I salute her for picking up the pieces. Good for her as everything in her garden is lovely now. People salute her and her money and she is making hay while the sun continues to shine and smile on her.

'You ain't seen anything yet babes. Delhi hides more in its bosom than that woman does. The secrets will reveal themselves in good time. Meanwhile, relish the champagne wishes and the caviar dreams. It's no longer love or money as it was when we were growing up; it's only love for money, now that is the single most important aspiration of all. I'm so glad I have Amit as my true friend. He keeps me in seventh heaven all day long and some nights too.' She giggled as she said this and turned to gaze dreamily into Amit's deep brown sex-starved eyes.

'He is a true friend with plenty of benefits,' Reema looked at me directly when she said this and broke into peals of laughter at my stunned expression. 'OMG! Look at your face. You look scandalized Zoya. I was just kidding. I'm not sleeping with Amit babes, I'm not mad.'

'I know you don't. I mean I know what kind of relationship you share with your hub. He means the world to you.' I responded while breaking into a girly giggle with her.

Tonight was the first of the 25 celebrations that Reema had promised when I reached Delhi. On average that would mean two celebrations a day as I was booked to return precisely two weeks later and I knew that it was the same with Natasha. I was certain that by the end of it I would have a book of anecdotes to share with my somewhat conservative friends back in London.

Tonight I would just try to experience Delhi through this place full of smoke and mirrors; metaphorically as well as literally.

7

Now we were the Three Amigos once again and we were about to re-unite with the fourth at the restaurant later; Vick had promised to join us at the restaurant. I was looking forward to his customary chuckle, which I was sure was how he would greet me. He had the innate ability to bring a smile to a face; even if it was wrought with tension. In this self-centred world, this quality was really refreshing.

We chatted and chuckled endlessly by Reema's poolside just like we did once upon a time. There had been torrential rain the night before due to which the lawns were wet and mucky but the air was cool and clear enough to do our breathing exercises. For Reema it was normal practice to do her *Pranayama* — yoga-breathing exercises — every morning followed by some stretches.

I simply stretched my hand for another toast and requested Shamji, the hero in my life in Delhi, for another *masala* tea in the largest mug in the kitchen. Fortunately, Reema disregarded my request and turned to Natasha instead to teach her exercises that would energise her.

Natasha was anything but lethargic. She was fresher than the farm air, considering that she only reached home at 4 a.m. and chatted with us till 6 a.m.

She was raring to go even though it was just 9 a.m. and I just about rolled out of bed to have my morning tea with them. The humidity was rising and I wished I could have my next cuppa in my air-conditioned bedroom while I completed the final chapter of John Grisham's *Abduction*.

'Girls, we are going for brunch with the family as soon as Sandy and Arun return from the golf course, so get your skates on! Smart casual is the dress code and being a Sunday we are bound to bump into half of Delhi so wear your best smiles. I ensure my smile is always sparkling by getting my teeth whitened every six to eight months. My dentist is just awesome and he is young and hot who longs to get his teeth into my mouth,' she chortled. Natasha and I rolled with laughter in our chairs.

Sandy was a good father. He taught golf to both his boys and had been teeing off with them every Saturday and Sunday morning, at the crack of dawn, for the past few years. Varun had, off late, taken a rain check owing to mounting pressure in school and his determination to make the grade. His high grades would be his passport to the ultimate freedom of leaving home for a few years to explore the other side. Besides, it was the usual practice with Delhi children in this financial bracket to study abroad. The exposure presumably did good for their self-confidence and expectantly gave their life a meaningful direction.

Reema had her heart set on the La Piazza restaurant at the Hyatt Hotel for a Sunday buffet brunch. It was heaving, by the time we reached, and thankfully Reema's personal secretary had made an early reservation. We had a large round table to ourselves.

Natasha and I were the only two heads that were up glancing around to soak in the pleasant ambience of this Italian restaurant. Its simple earthy décor was quite breathtaking. We exchanged words of approval as well as pleasantries with acquaintances who came to our table. Reema and Sandy were an integral part of the elite coterie and were known to many. Reema greeted everybody with a bright smile, revealing her blindingly white teeth. Sandy's teeth were just as white and sparkling. I wondered if he too went to the same dentist. A few minutes after settling down, the entire family had their heads down on their BlackBerrys and iPhones. We may as well text each other rather than attempt a conversation, I thought. No one spoke for a few extended minutes; the boys were either texting or playing games on their phones, Sandy was perhaps sending business e-mails and Reema was clearly messaging someone, as she wore a faint smile on her face. This was the new-age family lunch. Mobiles were both a boon and a curse. They were a means of communication, growing in numbers by the day — yet people were notably out of touch.

Within minutes, I realised, to my amazement, that the diners on the other tables too had their fingers punching buttons on their mobiles.

The younger of Reema's sons, Arun, was particularly cute. Each time Natasha or I asked him a question, he would look up momentarily, offer a broad smile that showed his braces and then perhaps on realising how conspicuous they were, would abruptly seal his lips, smile and then bury his head back into his game. His already rosy cheeks would flush even further and both Reema and Sandy would give him an endearing glance.

I secretly wished for Vick to hurry as his presence may just bring some energy to the surroundings.

Natasha had a look of amusement on her face as I mused that from a distance. Our Facebook friends send kisses, hugs, smiles and all sorts of icons and when we were with them they find it so difficult to express themselves. Had the mechanical expressions taken over the real feelings? Most people I met so far, only air kissed.

This trip to Delhi was also an opportunity to get reacquainted with Natasha. I was once again reminded about how perceptive she was; making clear observations about people from reading their expressions. She knew how to handle those she loved and didn't allow being mishandled by those she didn't. All her life, she had broken the rules to stand up for what she believed in. Societal norms in the '80s were regimented; girls studied till 21, got married at 22, had the first child by 23 and by 24 were well-versed in being a homemaker, mother, daughter-in-law and a wife. There was no need to look beyond the four walls of her marriage. Before society compelled her to live by its rules, she set her own, and flew to Paris. What was termed as rebel then is termed regular today so she jumped into an era that was just around the corner for women anyway. Our grandmas may be turning in their graves to see the kind of radical change we are seeing of late, but some of the so-called impediments, to equal opportunity for women, just had to be taken out of the way.

I admired Natasha then and I have high regard for her today as she has earned a lot of respect as a journalist. She wrote on trends and events related to culture — arts, fashion and entertainment and also more serious issues. I had recently come across an article of hers on how social and economic changes are affecting today's generation. What made her a good journalist is that she had strong opinions on things that matter and was not afraid to voice them. She was confident and had a charisma that went beyond her pretty, youthful face.

I could see the growing frustration on her face; she was obviously as irritated as I was with the maddening silence of the people around us and the deafening sound of the gadgets. She could no longer hold her tongue.

'So Reema, let me know the game plan once you have a moment from your first love; your mobile. In case you find it easier, you could BBM me the plans for the next two weeks.'

Reema apologised for being preoccupied and spoke in her usual everything-is-under-control attitude. 'Girls, we are leaving for Goa this Friday; the three of us for sure and Vick still has to confirm. I've arranged everything — from the flights and the hotel pick-up to the itinerary in Goa and finally the return on Monday night. It's all set in stone girls and we are set to have a party.'

I looked at Sandy as he watched her discuss her Goa plans. I couldn't help but wonder why he wasn't included in any of the plans considering he was the one who tied the knot with her all those years ago. Wasn't that the reason for all of us to be here together; to celebrate their togetherness, which I must admit I had hardly witnessed so far. But I chose not to say anything, as I didn't want to blow the fuse on something I had been sensing since my arrival.

'I'm leaving for Mumbai first thing Thursday,' announced Sandy, as if covering up for the embarrassment at not being made a part of the plan. 'I am also planning to make a quick trip to Thailand, for a couple of days, before the big bash. I have kept to my end of the bargain by making all the arrangements but if there's still anything that needs doing let me know before I go.'

I had been noticing that there was hardly any eye contact between Sandy and Reema even though they sat directly opposite each other. The boys still had their heads down and exchanged words with each other intermittently.

'Vick won't be joining us I'm afraid as he is spending the afternoon with his mother.' Reema announced after reading a text from her mobile. Natasha and I expressed our disappointment.

Sandy smirked at this and I wondered why. Natasha, unlike me, was more outspoken and unhesitatingly asked Sandy to share the joke.

'The kids are on the table so I would rather keep it zipped,' said Sandy rather calmly, though that triggered a torrential storm from Reema.

'What bullshit! You are the last person who knows how to keep it zipped. In fact, I don't think your trousers

have an f*****g zip,' snapped Reema. Her voice was a few
notches higher than usual, and then to our horror, she lost
control of her tongue. The presence of the children didn't
seem to bother her as she verbally attacked Sandy. She was
obviously angry and was quite incoherent. Just a few stray
words, like negligence, work, time seeped through to our
comprehension.

'Hold your tongue Reema. We have guests and the
children at the table. I don't know what you are referring to.
Maybe you and I can have a chat later, in the privacy of our
home. What do you say? For now let's all enjoy the meal,'
Sandy suggested coolly.

Sandy was clearly concerned about keeping up appearances
whilst Reema couldn't care less. She looked as if she was ready
to wrestle it out with him at the table. She was seething with
rage. I must say her behaviour was out of character and took
us by complete surprise, but Natasha and I decided to not
comment here.

The large succulent pizzas had arrived along with the
salads and the pastas so we buried our heads in the food.
I suddenly found myself getting into stress eating with all the
carbs on my plate while Natasha calmly settled on the salad.
Our heads were bowed down very close to the plates.

But Reema clearly was not pacified at Sandy's earlier
attempt to keep things calm.

'You need to stop judging my friends and instead
look in the mirror to see what you have become. At least
my friends are loyal to their partners and those who are

married respect the sanctity of the union. You can't even spell fidelity, let alone grasp its f*****g meaning. You are too busy grasping other things so don't even talk about zipping it baby! You are incapable of fidelity as you are of honesty,' yelled Reema at Sandy.

And then all hell broke loose.

Suddenly, I much preferred getting back to the moment when everyone was busy with their respective mobiles. Technology had evolved but clearly people hadn't. At least there was peace and quiet when the gadgets had taken over. My pizza got stuck in my mouth and the boys dug their heads deeper into their games. Their hands reached out for their plates without looking at it.

Reema was scathing, 'Vick is a loyal friend and has a right to chose his sexual orientation. Why do you always point your fingers at my friends? I know that the arrival of Natasha and Zoya also bugged the living daylights out of you, but you hid it well. You are always viewed as the nice guy and don't want to endanger that, but baby you and I know better, because I have had the misfortune to live with you and to endure your hypocrisy. I just hope I don't have to do this much longer. The sun is going to set on our marriage very soon baby.'

It was apparent that Sandy was desperate to maintain his decorum before us. Even if he was angry, he was too well-mannered to show it. 'Reema, baby, I really don't know what your issue is. I love Natasha and Zoya and don't forget I am the one who had the rooms renovated before their arrival and decided to give you space by staying with my parents in

Westend. I have even given you my BMW and now presumably I will be paying for your Goa trip as well, which I didn't even know was being planned. Have I ever complained about your incessant bills and the fact that you haven't amended your lifestyle inspite of the recession? You are clueless about the real world and live in your bubble. How can you judge me? And as for infidelity, let's not even go there because if we do then skeletons will come tumbling out of the closet. You don't want that, do you Reema? Now let's try and enjoy our family lunch with or without your dear gay friend. And for God's sake I am not compelled to like all your bum-chum pals, am I?' He sniggered as he said this.

My straw got stuck on the roof of my mouth. I had never heard Sandy speak like this before. Natasha just let out a deep sigh as if to say 'must we go through this drama guys' and then rolled her eyes in exasperation.

Reema left the table in a huff. Varun followed her after making the comment that he had had enough and couldn't wait to have them out of his hair. Being a teenager, he was more disturbed by the fact that the drama had taken place before us. Cute and cuddly Arun just fixed his eyes on his game and refused to acknowledge the commotion around him. Children have the ability to make themselves inconspicuous in a situation that makes them uncomfortable. His chubby crimson cheeks did not express his true feelings. Sandy offered him another slice of pizza and Arun unhesitatingly took it. He made the smart decision to keep his mouth busy while the adults around him sorted their over-complicated lives out. In a quiet tone he requested his father to carry the leftovers home for Cleo. He obviously couldn't wait to get back home to the calmer company of the pug.

Sandy then turned towards us and said, 'I throw my hands up in the air beautiful ladies. I have left no stone unturned to give your friend every shred of happiness. Whatever she touches is hers. She wants the latest Hermés, Gucci, Prada, Louis Vuitton or whatever it is, is hers at the first glance. She carries my credit card like it's her soulmate. She throws lavish parties at the farm; with or without me. I had built it years ago with my hard-earned money for her and the kids to enjoy; a true labour of love if you ask me. She travels first class, stays in luxury hotels, shops till she drops. Just last week I ordered the new BMW M6 for her, to replace the old one. She already has the Aston Martin lying in the garage for the past two years. She never drives it so I use it from time to time. I bought her the Patek Phillipe last year and this year I bought the diamond-studded Cartier. For our anniversary, I have ordered her a six carat solitaire ring and she also insists that she needs a new diamond set for the big bash. Oh! For God's sake, what else can a man do to make his wife happy? I have slogged my ass off for her and the boys and she doesn't appreciate a dime. She only knows how to get on my case. I love her ladies but I don't understand her. The belief that men are from Mars and women are from Venus is absolutely true in our case. I am certain that Reema is from another planet. I always said that she was out of this world and she sure as hell looks it, with her regular botox and liposuctions.'

He broke into laughter, either because he genuinely found his own joke funny or he was trying to conceal an underlying emotion that was far from funny. 'Her cosmetic surgeon is my friend so I know exactly the amount she spends on her appearance.'

It was difficult to believe that they were the same blessed, happy couple of the '80s; when their love story could be compared to a fairy tale. It was also a time when every dime was appreciated and people were respected more than objects.

Sandy then gave me a pleading look and said, 'Zoya, you are a very balanced lady and I respect you. Why don't you try and talk some sense into your friend. She doesn't listen to me anymore. She's lost touch with everything that was once important for us. I don't want to lose her. I really love her.'

Then he turned his gaze to Natasha, bringing her into the conversation, and said, 'I have never loved any other woman beside Reema. She is the one for me and always will be. Please make her see some sense. Perhaps this is the reason why you guys have returned to Delhi after so many years; to save our marriage. Damn it! Our anniversary is just a farce. We don't have a marriage. Her so-called friends in Delhi are all a bad influence on her. Look at Vick for God's sake, what advice can he give her. And look at Tina; after an acrimonious divorce she sleeps with every other industrialist to climb her way up the corporate ladder and her other friend Sarita, who is married but openly screwing her trainer. What kind of guidance can they offer her? Useless buggers.'

I must admit that I did feel sorry for Sandy as once upon a time we were the thick of friends, who understood each other and stood by each other. Sandy was sensitive and caring, even though he had the charm and charisma of Sean Connery. He had retained his style and came across as a man of character, his oodles of humor notwithstanding, but today's far-from-amenable lunch made me realise that there was obviously much we did not know — that appearances might be deceptive.

Something had obviously gone completely wrong between Reema and Sandy and both Natasha and I knew that it would be unfair to intervene without getting a clearer picture. While I said this in my mind, Natasha did not hesitate to voice it out, 'Sandy, I believe that in a marriage no partner has the right to upset the other the way we were just witness to. I need to understand what is going on before I play the mediator.'

I put on a blank expression to cover the multitude of speculations racing through my head, while Natasha just sat up straighter; an indication that she would not change her mind. Sandy just shrugged his shoulders before he looked at the waiter, with commanding eyes, for the bill.

8

Vick met us at the Diva restaurant in Greater Kailash Market Two. He was good-looking at five feet seven inches height; well-toned, well-groomed and everyone's sweetheart. He could be particularly sensitive to women.

'Yesterday's lunch was a disaster honey,' Natasha said after greeting him warmly. 'I know Reema was chatting with you over the phone last night. She was so upset that we just stayed in and watched her sulk and sob. You know how Reema is; so strong and yet so sensitive. She cried and cursed and cleaned up all her drawers as a way of venting out. She actually threw away bags full of clothes, shoes and handbags. My heart was sinking, as I watched all the branded stuff going into junk bags for charity. I was just dying to dig my hand into the bags for a lucky dip.'

'I know, I know. Well at least anger turns her into a guardian angel by getting her to do charity, so, for her at least, it's a great emotion,' laughed Vick, before asking, 'Where is she anyway?'

'In the loo,' I responded.

Vick had become more gorgeous with age. I wondered what it was with single men that kept them ever youthful and

young. Was it the fact they had no family responsibilities —
a hassled spouse, harassing kids or hefty bills. I wish time
was kinder to single women. I was in my mid-forties and
most certainly couldn't trick myself or others into believing
otherwise, as I looked every inch my age. My weight had also
begun to bother me, reminding me every second how much
I needed to lose. Here in Delhi, Reema kept a close check on
my calories. Back home it was a different story altogether. My
higher self then nudged and reminded me not to be superficial
and to age gracefully, notwithstanding the botox and other out
of the ordinary options available to turn back the clock.

Reema walked to the table after an extended time in the
washroom. My guess was that she had been on the phone
which I had aptly dubbed as her first love.

'Hey babes,' she said, hugging Vick. 'I'm pissed off today.
My better half is making me feel really bitter.' She laughed as
she said this.

I had been noticing that both Sandy and Reema laughed
at their own jokes. Perhaps marriage had taught them to
preserve their sense of humour since everything else was
evidently falling apart.

'Anyway guys, we are not going to waste our Monday
bitching about my husband who is becoming increasingly
belligerent. It's quite an achievement for having shacked up
with him for 25 years and that must be celebrated with a
bang. Like they say guys, if you can't cure it you must endure
it. Now let's decide the game plan.'

'What do you have in mind?' We all asked in unison.

But my curious mind couldn't help but pick up her use of the word *belligerent* to speak about Sandy. What had he done to hurt her? I'm sure Natasha also noticed Reema's use of this word but she chose to overlook it.

'Well, we are going to spend the weekend in Goa that's for sure. Natasha and Zoya are in one room and I have my own because I need my privacy. As for you Vick, I need my guy to make a reservation for you, as I wasn't sure about your plans. We are going to have the time of our lives and girls. We pack light with our bikinis and skimpy dresses that grab the attention of saucy and spicy men.'

'Sounds like a wet and wild plan. Now let's order some nosh, my eager beaver friends. I'm famished as usual. How's the fish out here Reema?' I intervened, as it was hunger as usual for me.

'Fish is good and let's have it with plenty of greens. Zoya, babes I want you to squeeze into the orange and gold bikini I gave you that I picked up from Bali recently. Eat light. No dessert for you at all. Vick, you're vegetarian so you order your pasta with greens babes.' Reema suggested in her typical commanding tone, as one who had everything under control. 'Natasha, you are eternally slim and superb looking so you can eat everything. How lucky.'

'I'll have very little, since I had a heavy South Indian breakfast and besides, I need to watch my weight too. I might not be wearing a bikini on the beach but I will be wearing my sexy trunks,' Vick said and chuckled before adding, 'Reema will you be going for the salsa class tonight?'

'No babes I'm cancelling it tonight. I've informed my dance partner, Amit. Varun needs me to help fill in the application forms for universities because we have a meeting tomorrow with his counsellor. Are you going Vick?'

'Ok! Ok! No Reema, I broke off with Sahil, my dance partner, or life partner as I considered him. A part of me hurts but a greater part of me is relieved since he was always stoned. I just couldn't handle him anymore.' He then continued, 'You know guys, my prayer to God has always been, "hand me anything and I'll handle it," but Sahil was too much. He was a handful.' He broke into a roaring laughter first and joined him in chorus. We were the loudest diners in the restaurant and invited many curious glances.

He then continued in a more serious tone. 'I definitely want to be part of the plan Reema as I think it will do me and my broken heart a lot of good. I must admit that I do miss Sahil even though I know he wasn't the right one for me. But then who is right? I mean love is so conditional nowadays. His name, tattooed on my shoulder, has now become a burden. I feel like a fool now with *Sahil* written all over me. The guys on the beach may assume that I'm already hooked. Oof! So annoying! Maybe I should get another tattoo next to it saying *Ex*.'

Vick was hilarious and inspite of his obvious heartache we could not help but laugh as he discussed his love life and how things had gone terribly wrong. He had been in relationships with a series of men who had chosen to be with him merely because he was well-off and always pampered his partners by buying things for them and taking them to exotic destinations outside India. He eventually awakened to the unfortunate truth that he was not the one they prized, but his wealth.

'When I first met Sahil I wanted to shout from the rooftops that I loved him, but then I lost him. I've been unlucky in love. I was smitten and made him the centre of my existence and now he's left a huge void in my life that I just don't know how to fill,' said Vick sadly.

'Fill it with fun and games. What else? What do you need? A letter of approval from your parents? Each one of us is a naughty forty, so come on, don't think, just do. Action baby action! Who knows, you may just find the love of your life on the beach. Don't give up. I haven't. My marriage passed its sell-by date years ago and I may not have the title of a *miss* anymore, but I still have the right to love,' insisted Reema.

'Miss-guided hun. That's what you are,' laughed Natasha as we all joined in, in good spirit.

'I will let you know by tomorrow, first thing. But you know I was wondering if anyone wants to catch up on a movie tonight. We could go to the Director's Cut for a complete movie experience. It should be fun.' Vick offered enthusiastically.

'Why don't you take Natasha and Zoya? I'll catch up with you guys later at the farm, for dinner. I'll get the cooks to make some great Chinese food; chicken, tofu, broccoli, pak choy and all the other wholesome greens. How does that sound? And please don't eat junk at the cinemas; especially you Zoya. I know you just love your nachos with cheese but it's time to head for the machos now. I'm going to make sure you shed off a few kilos before you head back to London. I mean it babes. You are going to be hot and make heads turn and hearts churn. Remember that was always our motto. Nothing has changed. Natasha you and I are going to hook up Zoya for sure in these two weeks and I know just the guy who would love to bed you. In fact we are all in our prime guys and we need to look as hot as Charlie's Angels, except we don't need to be angels.' Reema responded and broke into peals of laughter.

'Honey, I would rather be the devil that wears Prada and believe me if I set my eyes on a cute guy then I'll drop everything, literally down to nothing,' roared Natasha. 'So honey, before hooking up Zoya, who you think needs to swallow the greens to bring out her sheen, you better hook me up. I'm always game.'

'Okay guys, let's just rewind to the movie. I need to arrange the tickets so please confirm, like now,' reminded Vick.

Natasha responded, 'I don't particularly have a penchant for late night movies, but hey why not? All of us together will be fun. Reema you see how you're placed after filling in the forms. If you're done early, then come and join us honey. It will do you good to distract your mind.'

'Yes!' I intervened. 'Take it as part of your 25-years-celebrations. We'll all wear black and do our eye make-up dramatically and paint the town red.'

'No seriously guys, I'm not going to be part of the fun and games, but keep a seat for me, just in case. Or else I'll see you guys back at the farm after the movie.' Reema responded emphatically.

'What about my eye make-up guys? Who's going to eye me up?' asked Vick, fluttered his eyelashes dramatically. He then rang up his secretary to book four tickets.

As we settled down with our food, with me determined to clear my serving and Reema just pushing her food around the plate, I noticed that she was once again busy with her mobile. We all were getting accustomed to the fact that Reema's phone was an extension of her body, so we just ignored the incessant tapping.

She finally placed her mobile down. The rest of the lunch was fun; we spoke about the bygone days, falling in and out of love, our work and workouts and the changing times that we were trying to keep pace with in our own respective ways — all in all revelling in the fact that in today's society our friendship had remained constant, despite the fact that we were separated by continents.

We concluded our lunch with a hot chocolate fudge cake; of which I had the lion's share despite Reema watching over me like a hawk.

'C'mon Reema! We are celebrating a reunion after a decade. You cannot deprive me of just a little indulgence,' I said, flashing my most angelic smile, which may not have been as impressive as her sparkling one but for now it seemed to do the trick.

Rolling her eyes, she reached for her spoon, for just one bite. The others too had a teaspoonful each. As for me, I could never settle on a single bite; it was all or nothing for me.

We spotted an old friend of ours a few tables away, sitting with a young, skimpily dressed white girl who was most certainly not his wife. He had noticed us too, but was trying to pretend otherwise. His hands were gliding audaciously across her thighs and under her skimpy skirt. Reema was amused and told us that his wife had put on some weight. That had given him the excuse to have flings. Apparently Reema often bumped into Rohan and each time he was with a new hot chick.

Gosh! I thought whilst taking in another bite; yet another guy who feels the need to have his cake and eat it too.

9

Delhi has a distinct smell during the monsoon season that is almost intoxicating. And when it rains it definitely pours. The heavy downpour, at times, makes the umbrella absolutely useless for those attempting to walk. However, it can be an exciting time for some; it is not uncommon to see urchins and pavement dwellers dancing in the rain while singing popular Bollywood tunes.

I personally became poetic and connected well to my inner being, whatever that may be, as the rain drenched everything around me.

At this moment however, our car was stuck in the worst traffic jam anyone can imagine as we drove over the Greater Kailash flyover, through Panchsheel Park, to the Vasant Vihar flyover. We had been glued to the same spot for the past 20 minutes now. The movie now seemed like a distant dream, with the rain threatening to play spoilsport. There was chaos on the roads as the city is never prepared for heavy showers; apart from the cars, street vendors, rickshaw *wallah*s, sweepers, cleaners, beggars and urchins were all trying to go about their tasks, while trying to save themselves from the incessant downpour. The cows on the road also appeared to have a purpose and they walked steadily and surely on whichever side suited them. They knew all too well that they were considered sacred hence took the liberty of strolling on any side they wanted, while moving cars usually waited with patience till they crossed over. Reckless trucks and buses are known to have run over people on Delhi roads without an ounce of remorse, but the emotion for the holy cow has always been different. Human life had always been cheap out here.

The ice-cream vendors were particularly busy with kids from schools in that locality. Tagore International, DPS and Modern School were all located where our car was trapped. Fruit and vegetable vendors were selling their wares to women who were haggling on every rupee; driven by sheer habit. They got a thrill out of bringing down the price, not realising that the vendor had probably hiked it up anyway knowing what was in store for him at the market; all this in spite of the rain.

The crowded roads and sidewalks were always entertaining for onlookers; particularly for me as back in London I could not see this diversity. The contrast between the rich and the poor was extreme here, but every individual had his own rich tale to tell.

I wondered momentarily how I could not but miss this most colourful canvas, although when I stayed here, I probably did not even notice this variety of life around me.

The traffic on the roads too had changed; it was no longer just the locally manufactured cars with the odd imported cars but the Toyotas, Hondas, Skodas, BMWs, Mercedes, Porsches, Bentleys, Lamborghinis and Ferraris that ruled the roads. I realised that what I was witnessing now was the emergence of new wealth. A few beggars and urchins knocked on our window pleading for money to buy food but I had no change and Natasha turned the other way.

'I wrote a whole article on this and I don't wish to fall prey to this kind of behaviour. They will coax you if you are not careful honey. Try and understand the money is not for food hun. Just look the other way if you cannot say no,' she advised strictly.

'I'm feeling parched. Are there any water bottles in the car?' I asked Reema's chauffeur.

'Yes Ma'am,' came the prompt response and he told me where I would find the water bottle.

'New York isn't this bad,' compared Natasha. 'It rains there too but doesn't bring the traffic to a halt. Road clogging is unheard of out there and London is also notorious for its rains but even there the traffic doesn't come to a standstill. Delhi is so modern and yet lacks the infrastructure to handle this yearly breakdown.'

'This is what I detest about Delhi; the choked traffic, the deafening hooting that is like a soundtrack playing all day long, and the undercurrent of aggression in the people in their screeching cars. Road rage seems to be more prevalent here than in the West. It's terrible.' I commented as I observed two people, right in front of our car, one on his motorbike and the other in his car, yelling obscenities at each other. Within minutes, other passers-by joined in to add fuel to the fire, to yell out *bhen***** and *ma*****, which rolled off their tongues as easily as *Yo* slides off the tongues of the youth today. In fact, the BC and MC words were not just used as abuses but had become an integral part of conversations between people — usually men.

The finest example would be… 'That *bhen***** car is superb *yaar*! It *bhen***** runs at the speed of lightening and *bhen***** I'm going to buy it with my dad's money and while I'm at it I'm *bhen***** going to buy myself a Versace coat in which I'll look *bhen***** hot man. My life *bhen***** rocks…' I personally took the literal meaning and was deeply distressed on hearing it until I understood its wider use and in a much broader context just like the word f**k is used in the English language.

I joked and asked Natasha, 'Pass me the *bhen***** water. I wish the *bhen***** traffic would move and the people would stop dilli-delhi-ing!'

On the road the word *bhen***** was still synonymous with rage. I noticed that an already bad situation had become irreparable because of the unnecessary intervention of the bystanders. Why on earth did everyone decide to battle it out just ahead of our car?

Natasha was amused at my use of the BC word.

'We seem to be a magnet for aggression,' she laughed. 'Do you think it was actually a good idea to come to India; I mean with the tension between Sandy and Reema. Personally, I didn't even know that there were any problems between them. I clearly remember them as a well-settled couple, very much in love. But I suppose love has become a shaky and unreliable emotion. I'm not sure I feel comfortable being around, what with the strain between them.'

I agreed with her, 'I'm not sure if this trip to India was such a smart idea but if nothing else we can enjoy Goa together and perhaps even encourage Sandy to join us there. At the end of the day he is a great guy. Remember all the fun we used to have all those years ago? We would hop from one nightclub to the other and the respective managers would lay out the red carpet for him. Even back then he had a princely charm and the means to flaunt it and Reema was his one and only princess. How has time changed them or is it that Delhi itself has changed quite drastically?'

'Delhi was fab back then, honey,' shrieked Natasha in excitement as she began to reminisce. 'Those were the good old days. Seems like just yesterday when we boogied in Gunghroo, followed by an evening at Number One, and My Kind of Place. There was one particular song that springs to mind from that era. Do you remember it?'

'Which one love? *Brother Louie* by Modern Talking. OMG! I loved it! We all danced to it — you, Reema and I. What fun we had.'

'Yessssss! I can dance to it right now,' said Natasha.

'Brother Louie Louie Louie...' was playing in my head and then it just wouldn't stop. For a few moments I was transported back to that time, space and sensibility.

'Oh! Where has it all gone? Where does it all go anyway? It seems like just yesterday. But so much time has gone by...

Hey, and then there was "You're My Heart, You're My Soul",' screamed Natasha, remembering the old times.

Our minds switched between the past and the present. The new replaces the old and that is the circle of life. Suddenly, I missed having Kwality ice-cream at India Gate, from the street vendors, and then going for *chaat* in Bengali Market; the unhygienic way in which the vendor would serve the *gol gappas* perhaps enhanced the flavour, and on eating it we would all say in chorus, '*Yummy, yummy; bad for my tummy!*' We would relish every bite and at times have Delhi Belly for the next few days. Later on, Nirula's came into existence and eating there would be a tireless thrill. My all-time favourite became the salad bar followed by the Gulabo ice-cream and 21 Love. That was the sort of fun that filled our days; innocent and inexpensive. Most importantly, we knew the value of everything big and small and cherished the people with whom we shared them.

The new reality of modern Delhi, as per my observation so far and what I had heard from Reema and Vick, was a city that had become shallow and indifferent to life's simple pleasures. People were in a mad rush to become a somebody or to at least know somebody who would help them achieve what they were aspiring for.

'Could somebody get us out of this mess. What's the name of that minister who Reema knows?' asked Natasha, echoing my thoughts. 'She said she generally called her from the road to get her out of mayhem like this. I'm going to call Reema up.'

Reema didn't take her call. She must be busy with Varun and his paper work. Besides, a few minutes later the end-of-the-world drama was over, the road cleared as the traffic policeman came to the rescue. He too yelled obscenities at the people, slapped and abused the man on the scooter and profusely apologised to the man in the car. The bigger man wins, I mused.

Vick had reached before us and we all headed up the escalator of Ambience Mall in Vasant Kunj.

The multiplex was ultra luxurious and I hadn't encountered anything like this before. It was so quiet inside; a far cry from what we had encountered on the streets outside.

As we were ushered to our seats for the movie, I thought I saw a figure I recognised. The lights were dim and the movie had just started so without further ado we sat on our most comfortable seats. I immediately leaned back on the reclining seat and opened the packet that contained a fresh blanket. The novelty of watching a movie lying down, as I would in my living room, was overwhelming; something that I was experiencing in Delhi for the first time.

'Ultra luxury,' stated Natasha. 'Do you do this often Vick? It's nothing like any other movie experience. I could just doze off as I'm already drained from the terrible traffic we had to push through.'

That is precisely what she did. Thirty minutes into the movie and Natasha was sound asleep. Vick and I chatted in hushed tones throughout the movie; cracking jokes about this and that and then I finally succumbed to the nachos instead of the machos that Reema was on the lookout for, for me. I made Vick promise that he wouldn't tell Reema.

I knew that she abhorred junk food just as passionately as I adored it.

It was at the interval that I finally recognised the figure I could not discern in the dark. He had sprinted down the stairs and into the foyer with a young girl and I decided to follow him.

'Varun! What are you doing here? I thought you were filling forms tonight for your universities?' I enquired.

Even if Varun was taken aback by my presence, he remained unfazed. I could read brazenness in his stare, as though he was daring me to reprimand him for being at the movies, instead of poring over his books. But then he suddenly seemed to realise something and his expression changed, 'Is mom with you? She obviously is right?'

I told him that she wasn't.

I stood in a queue to order salted popcorn. I asked Varun if he would like anything, besides a lesson in manners. The latter I kept to myself though I was dying to shake him from his arrogance. I wondered if they made humble pills that I could pop into the Diet Pepsi he was sipping on. Nothing wrong in being cool, but the arrogance was abhorrent.

Reema was not with her son so where was she? What was she up to? I could feel myself burning with curiosity.

Oh! For God's sake… I told my over-imaginative head. I wasn't here to judge my friend but to commemorate her 25th wedding anniversary. But then we should be celebrating with her and not watching a film that none of us were actually interested in; Natasha was actually snoring right through.

If I shared my concern for Reema with Natasha she would surely choose to confront Reema with this and thus put the celebration and our years of friendship into jeopardy. So I considered silence to be golden. Zip it. I said to myself... Mum is the word.

As I was going back inside the auditorium, Varun gently patted me on the back. 'Please don't tell mum that you saw me here... I was to study at a friend's place and she doesn't know about my girlfriend. It's a long story, you know what I mean? It's kinda complicated. Can you keep quiet? Please,' pleaded Varun, as I popped in several popcorns into my mouth. 'As for filling in forms, we did that weeks ago; so I don't know where that's coming from... but please aunty. I beg of you.'

Aha! The rolls of attitude were now rolling away as I had the upper hand. Nice. I was cherishing every moment of this.

'Uh! Let me see. Are you enjoying the film? How about your friend?'

'Aunty, please,' begged Varun.

Now he was looking serious as he continued, 'Life at home is already quite unbearable and whatever mom and dad do is excused, but I will just be adding fuel to the inferno if they find out I am out with my girlfriend. Please aunty, you've seen nothing yet as they both are in their best behaviour. There are fireworks at home every night and it's my grandparents who come and diffuse the situation; not that they are respected. Honestly, they are treated like they are just coming in the way. Things are really bad. Trust me you ain't seen anything yet.'

'I'm just kidding Varun. I obviously won't say anything.' I reassured him and patted his back; I could understand his emotional state. Reema and Sandy weren't realising the repercussions their behaviour was having on the children. These were the impressionable years and what the kids saw or heard would determine their own behaviour and attitude. In today's day and age it was important to be the right role model for the kids.

I could not concentrate on the movie post interval. All I could think about was Reema. I realised that her Facebook photographs did reveal her crumbling love story; when we had all joined, early 2007, she would upload mushy photos of Sandy and her, and then with their two boys. Of late, it was just her at a charity ball or other social and cultural events — Sandy's photos were never uploaded.

I was angry with Reema for she had never spelt out that her marriage had developed cracks. We had often spoken about marriages breaking up; she had shared stories about the acrimonious divorces of some of her acquaintances, on the grounds of adultery and how growing insecurity in marriages was making women get nose jobs and boob jobs done.

With this came the unsettling thought about Amit and her. What was she really doing with him?

I realised that my closest friend was wearing a mask with me; to digest this after 30 years of friendship was a little difficult.

10

'He was on my list of *50 things to do in the evening*. So I met him. It was a casual chat over coffee babes. What's the big deal?' Reema responded at breakfast the following morning. She was clearly someone who was willing to push her boundaries and stand up for what she wanted; something that now defined her personality.

Natasha had decided to sleep in late, so it was just the two of us.

Reema was now typing swiftly on her iPad organising something related to her big anniversary bash. Then her mobile rang and she rolled her eyes, and reluctantly took the call. 'Yes? Yes! Yes! It's done!' She said in a curt tone before disconnecting the call and turning towards me said, 'That was marriage as usual. Now let's get down to pleasure as usual. My 25th anniversary bash. We will rock babes,' said Reema with a big smile. From what I had been able to gauge about her marriage, I wondered what the celebration was all about.

Dismissing these thoughts, I feigned an enthusiastic reply, 'Of course we will, love. That's why we are all here. What you doing on your iPad?' I asked curiously.

'Babes I run my entire life from this extraordinary device. I make notes, read, play Angry Birds and check my email and Facebook too; that's how we are all together again. Recently, I also set up my Twitter account. I remember my mother, in the '70s, learning typing and shorthand. Do you remember sending a telex? How simple is communication now.'

'Simply complicated...' This is what I wanted to say... Very few really know the meaning of communication these days. It's all so mechanical; emotions are expressed so easily on the device but are becoming increasingly difficult to express face-to-face. I wonder how an icon or a symbol has come to substitute the real thing and yet it momentarily brings a smile to our face whenever we receive it.

It was morning, but the dark clouds threatened rain as they enveloped the farm in a grey gloom.

'So where did you meet Amit yesterday?' I finally asked, even though I knew I would get a response that would be half-fact and half-fiction.

Reema responded without hesitation. 'Babes, Varun cancelled on me last minute and I would run very late if I joined you for the movie, so I went to Amit's apartment. We chatted and cracked jokes. He makes me happy babes. He's my best friend. That's it. No great shakes. Just friends.'

I looked around me; it would soon start raining heavily, and make it difficult for us to see the area around the farm clearly — much like how Reema was trying to create an ambiguous picture of the events of the previous evening. I knew the story she gave me was pure fiction.

I dared to voice my opinion, though very carefully, 'Reema, don't you think that you are weaving a really tangled web? I mean can I give you a third-party objective opinion about Amit and whatever is happening between you two?'

'Please Zoya, you are making a mountain out of a molehill. I mean there is nothing between us,' Reema snapped impatiently.

'Really Reema, I mean his hand was all over your yoga-tight ass, at the lounge bar, on the night of my arrival. And you were treating him as though he were a juicy piece of black pepper sirloin steak; ready for you to satisfy your appetite with. What am I saying? I mean, you shouldn't be with another man in the first place. Sandy is devoted to you, love. You are married remember? You are taking him for granted or are perhaps just bored, so you are seeking a short term, exciting and bumpy ride,' I said most agitatedly.

'Yuck! That's gross! Firstly babes, I maybe a strict non-vegetarian but I am a non beef-eating Hindu who would never consume a sirloin steak. Secondly, I don't consider Amit a juicy chunk of meat. I see him as my best friend and I'm not seeking any excitement with him and thirdly, and most importantly, let's close the topic right this very second because a little knowledge is a dangerous thing. Sandy is not devoted to me, but devoted to ruining my life. You know nothing, so let's change the subject,' Reema responded, her face reflecting her exasperation.

She ended the topic herself by adding, 'Tonight, Sameer is throwing a big bash at his farm. It's going to be awesome babes. The dress code is sexy glam. My maid Sarita will iron your clothes, so keep them out on your bed. If you need to visit the salon then join me at five in the evening. I'm going to Madonna in DLF Promenade. The owner is my friend, and then I need to pick up some tofu from Le Marche, that also belongs to her. You haven't been there yet. Its suuuper! They sell white tea and I want you to start on it.'

Reema obviously had no intention of heeding my advice on Amit and it annoyed me.

Even though I refrained from asking more questions or give her further advice, I mused over the kind of life Reema had chosen for herself. It was as if she was on the treadmill, not willing to pause and think about where she was heading. I had to admit though that she did look very happy with whatever route she had chosen for herself and she was moving on it at breakneck speed. It got me worried that by trying to fill every second of her life she was only moving into emptiness? With this also came the realisation that Amit may be nothing more than a transient fulfillment.

'Will Sandy be joining us love?' I dared to ask even though I already knew the answer. His absence would hardly be noticed, since she stole the show wherever she went. She was definitely a people's person radiating an aura that demanded attention; a woman of style with substance who had a strong sense of individuality.

'I guess he'll be joining us later, if at all. We'll leave by 10:30 p.m. babes, as I don't want to be too late. He has a pool too so we'll jump in later when there are just a few of us left.

What fun nah?' she chuckled, her face brightening up with an excitement which reminded me of the time I had known her as a teenager. Some events of our lives turn back the years for a few precious moments; then we go back to being a grown-up.

I must admit that I was most excited about meeting old friends and since Vick was going to accompany us we were sure to have a wonderful time, except that starting at 10:30 p.m. seemed ridiculously late. Gosh! I really had become a London girl as parties there began by 8:30 p.m. at best, which was much more true-to-life by my standards. My reality, however, was quite contrary to Reema's, but I told myself that life was all about meeting people mid-way in order to ensure harmony in relationships.

Natasha by now had woken up from her slumber and approached us at the poolside. She yelled at Reema, 'This humidity is making me sooooo lethargic. How do you brave the goddamn elements out here? I could sleep all day. Order some coffee for me, pleeeease, before I nod off again.'

'Sure babes! You need to wake up and get your skates on because life is a p-a-r-t-y and we are all going to let our hair down tonight... and whatever else we have to. After the bash we are going clubbing. Less is more guys so make sure your skin shows more than your dress. Dress to impress and make mess with any man who wants to undress with you,' Reema suggested, and we all rolled off our chairs with laughter, which totally got Natasha out of her lethargic stupor. She sat up to enquire about the guys who would be available at the party and Reema cattily informed that they were ALL ready to mingle, though not young, free and single. We all giggled again like teenage girls at the prospect of getting hooked up.

By now, I was sipping on my *masala* tea, Natasha was enjoying her coffee and Reema was taking generous gulps from her glass of fresh vegetable juice. As we relaxed in our comfortable chairs, I was soon lost in my own thoughts. The grand gazebo at the far corner of the farm caught my eye. I imagined Reema and Sandy standing beneath it — as they would next week — in their best attire, complete with their radiant smiles. They would gaze into each other's eyes and fall in love all over again. We friends would be celebrating their romance under the starry night.

I came out of my reverie to the sound of tinkling laughter; Reema had said something and both Natasha and she were laughing uproariously. I marveled at the contrast we represented; Reema in her short snow white nightdress, my hair in a half unkempt ponytail held together with a Minnie Mouse clip and Natasha with her pink Cinderella slippers on... a picture of innocence. And here we were together in the sprawling farm while partaking of Reema's ceaseless saucy tales about Delhi couples.

11

'Arun, baby, have you done your homework? Have you had your milk? Have you brushed your teeth? Are your pyjamas clean baby?' crooned Reema.

I watched his face as Reema fussed over him. He was probably thinking... The same stream of questions — everyday — seven days a week and the same time of the day... Don't mothers get bored hearing themselves make the same monotonous enquiries?

'Yes mom! Yes to your entire questionnaire mom,' responded Arun cheekily and Reema cuddled him like a baby, telling him how cute he was. They both giggled as she playfully tickled him. We watched the two in amusement. Cleo too had been watching them. He now joined in the fun by jumping onto the bed and lying on Arun's belly. He wanted to be tickled too, so Cleo got busy and Reema had to stop as she couldn't get to him anymore. Cleo had taken over and won. Arun looked happy as he was clearly very fond of Cleo. 'Mom I love you too, but I just love Cleo a little bit more,' he stated as he curved his index finger to join his thumb to show her just how much more he loved Cleo. Reema's eyes twinkled as she responded to him with a warm smile, which

I noticed was very different from the smiles she directed at her acquaintances. Arun was clearly her baby and she doted on him.

'I will always love you more than you love me baby and that's cool. All I want is for you to smile because that is what brightens my day and that of everyone in the house. Even Cleo is happy when you are happy. Practice smiling, everyday, before grandma; this will make her very happy and it will give her something to do everyday besides putting me down,' said Reema with a smile.

'But mom, I wear braces so my smile is not nice,' he pointed one of his little fingers at his teeth and continued, 'Mom, I do smile at grandma and grandpa, every morning, before going to school but they don't smile back at me if they have not worn their teeth which they keep in a glass by their bedside at night. So I get dis... dis... uh... What was that word you taught me to use instead of upset?'

'Disheartened, baby! Arun, it doesn't matter if you wear your braces or grandma and grandpa don't return your smile because they are not wearing their dentures. Your braces are temporary and I also had them while growing up, but your smile has to be a permanent fixture ok?' She chuckled as she said this. Arun truly made her happier than any other member of her family.

Reema believed she was a good mother who made sure that the boys ate, did their schoolwork, drank milk, brushed their teeth and smiled at all times. She wasn't a disciplinarian but she was regimented about certain things and that mounted to reasonably good upbringing. She wasn't a hands on mother since she herself was a busy bee, but she was definitely emotionally available for both her boys. They, in turn, were her lifelines.

'Arun! Please go to bed by 9 p.m. as you have school tomorrow baby and I don't want you to be late,' instructed Reema, and added, 'And Cleo please let my son sleep.'

As if Arun didn't know that he had school in the morning. But then again that was a mother repeating the same old dialogue — seven days a week, 52 weeks a year.

'Mom, Cleo sleeps with me! Remember! I wish he could go to school with me too, but then he doesn't need to as he is cleverer than all of us,' said Arun while stroking Cleo. 'My baby is the best.'

'Mom, can we go watch *Ice Age 4* tomorrow, after school?' asked Arun randomly, as children often do. Reema simply kissed him on the cheek and told him that they would take a call on that the next day.

After Arun had left, I told Reema that I needed to visit a few art galleries, particularly the one I was representing in London. There was an art show tomorrow evening at the Golf Links which Vick, Natasha and I were keen to attend. Bose Krishnamachari was showcasing his works. I could barely contain my excitement as I had sold a few of his paintings to my clients residing in Bishop's Avenue back in London and I was eager to meet the man himself. The evening was sure to get my creative juices flowing again and that was just what I needed more than consuming the fresh juices at Reema's farm.

'Babes, that sounds like a perfect plan but then we need a plan B that involves clubbing. Let's go to the Aman Hotel following the art show. It's only a stone's throw from there,' suggested Reema. 'But during the day I have my ladies kitty at the Leela Hotel and then the women's club meeting at the Hyatt for the preparation of the go-karting event for women in Noida, to be held next month. I'm inundated with social events babes. I'm skipping my personal training too as I'm pressed for time.'

Her phone beeped and she told us that it was a message from Varun, saying that he would be staying over at a friend's place to study.

'Oooof! What's wrong with my son? He's studying every waking minute. I'm so worried about his health. His diet goes for a toss since he starts eating junk outside. I think he's overdoing it,' commented Reema with a worried expression. Overdoing what, I wondered; as it definitely wasn't studying.

Later, with our hair and nails groomed for the night, Reema and I met Natasha and Vick, who had been strolling leisurely through the mall. We had also shopped at the most impressive Le Marche store that housed almost every food brand under the sun. I bought fresh lemon cheesecake. It was delectable and I pointed out to Reema that the cakes and pastries had most definitely improved since I left Delhi. Reema looked the other way as if I just commented on cocaine or weed or something. Maybe she would have responded to me if I had indeed commented the variety of narcotics easily available in the city now.

After getting pampered by a massage — done by a masseuse that Reema had called over — we showered and dressed up for the evening. When I lamented on how fat I looked, Vick pointed out, 'Zoya, you are Reema's friend, so they will love to rub shoulders with you regardless of your dress size, which you may have noticed was not a source of concern before you arrived here. You know that in Delhi high society, it's not who you are but who you know that counts. In addition, your address is London and that too central; so just chill and enjoy the party. Each of the Delhi parties is like a new released film, except with the same stars and the same plot, but with new flashy toys on wheels, watches and women. The same characters are involved but with different partners; in fact the partners may have just been swapped.

Reema interrupted him, 'You are just too funny Vick. Delhi is g-r-e-a-t and I l-o-v-e it! You can't paint the entire city with the same brush. It's just not fair. Come we need to leave now. Let's party tonight. I need to show off my new LV shoes and bag and my JJ Valaya ensemble. I love Delhi.'

'Of course, of course,' agreed Vick. 'Every place has its dark and brighter side and we need to only focus on the good. I was just kidding because I love Delhi. I mean who doesn't? I was just pointing out that the high society is an island that is governed by its own system,' said Vick.

'G-u-y-s,' screamed Reema. 'We can share all this philosophy once we are in the car. Come lets p-a-r-t-y.'

'Thank heavens we are finally leaving,' said Natasha. 'What time was the party supposed to begin hun? I'm already ready to doze off.'

'It's just 9:30 p.m. guys! That is Delhi standard time for parties, but no one turns up before 10:30. Let's go,' Reema yelled in excitement.

So we left at Delhi Stretch Time.

12

I was well acquainted with most of Reema's friends, from our old days, but I noticed now that they had changed most dramatically. There had been a simplicity and sincerity about them then, but they had now transformed into these well-groomed, polished individuals dressed up in apparels designed by renowned Indian and international designers; creating a complex personality that did not seem real to me. I realised that I had been away for a very long time; I could no longer figure them out.

The figure that was approaching us had a confident walk. The lady wore her attitude with the same assurance as she wore her short skin-tight, cleavage-showing gold sequinned dress. She positively knew she was a sex goddess. She delicately held onto her Birkin bag and I realised that the enormous rock on her delicate middle finger was probably heavier than her body weight. Her hair was long and lustrous and delicately brushed against her bosom to reach her waist. She clearly knew that beauty was power. I could not help wonder what could be going on in the mind of a woman who exuded this in-your-face sexiness. She probably knew that the bloom of beauty would be short-lived hence had decided to make the most of it while it lasted.

'Hey Natasha and Zoya, meet Esha who is a super mom with supermodel looks and is featured regularly on Page 3. Isn't she gorgeous? She is my best friend, Esha,' said Reema as she hugged her friend and went through the usual high-society party greeting; air kissing and excessive smiles and pleasantries. It made for the perfect photo moment which the professional photographers mingling amongst the guest, did not miss out.

Natasha, Vick and I exchanged looks with raised eyebrows as we wondered where we figured on Reema's *best friend* list. Vick commented that everyone who was a somebody in Delhi was always considered a best friend till someone bigger and better came along. After a while, Vick being Vick, whispered to Natasha and me that being on Page 3 these days was no great achievement since it only required paying the media on a monthly basis to get featured. These people made sure they were well-maintained with regular botox and other cosmetic treatments to appear good in print.

As for Esha, we learnt from Vick, that she was always busy with some job or the other; first she got a nose job, then a boob job last year, shortly after finding her new toyboy who was half her age and double her size; that was after she had dumped the previous love of her life who was quarter of a century older than her. These days she had no qualms about admitting that she preferred them younger; bigger and better, anatomically and materially.

'Money talks, dahlings, and it sometimes even screams, as in the case of Esha, who wears all her wealth on her fingers and lets them do all the talking. She just snaps her fingers and, in seconds, men are drooling all over her; abandoning their partners to lose themselves in Esha's plastic boobs and collagen smiles. By the way, her nickname is Mrs. Fendi because you walk into her home and you can see Fendi furnishing all over — it's like walking into a Fendi store,' chuckled Vick, before he continued, 'She has a personal dietician who keeps her on an anti-aging diet; an extortionate choice but it pays off, since she looks 10 years younger than her years and that is the reason why most of the men in her life are young too; one was as young as 22.'

'What about her husband, doesn't he say anything about the men and the money she squanders?' I asked naively.

'Money talks for him too Zoya and it gets him everywhere. What's good for the goose is good for the gander. They are both at it and in it together. They have a great understanding and I suppose that is how they keep their marriage going.

'Only the wise use their dosh with class and the rest are crass. Someone once said that *money talks and wealth whispers*; the nouveau riche of Delhi let their new money do almost all their talking and those with old wealth wouldn't be bothered about these social do's. Money makes up the very fabric of this society. You girls come back and stay here for good, get into great shape and you too could become the infamous elite socialites and get featured regularly in newspapers and magazines. Zoya, consider it darling, all that fame without being or doing anything of value. Actually that's not entirely true since some of the elite socialites are part of the eminent charity events and they raise funds to educate impoverished children in Indian villages. Pratham is an NGO that has been doing a lot of good work, since its beginning in Mumbai in the '90s. Esha, believe it or not, also raises funds and that is another reason for her to be featured regularly in newspapers and magazines like *Hello*, *Femina*, *L'Officiel* and others. Even Reema is part of this charity, Pratham, but rarely gets time to participate in its fund raising events. Besides, she has set up her own NGO. So you can say that there is good and not so good everywhere,' said Vick.

'Thank heavens, I only need my brain to remain in shape, to keep writing, and to make money,' laughed Natasha, and continued, 'And I get featured, rather my articles get featured in newspapers and magazines regularly. And thankfully, I do not need any corrective interventions for that.'

I laughed aloud, before adding, 'I am glad that I am only selling art in London and have not let my life become abstract. I colour my life's canvas with long-lasting shades.'

'As for me,' Vick added, 'I love the kaleidoscope of Delhi high society; its colourful, read sensational, ways that always fill my palette with exciting and shocking hues.'

We laughed out aloud.

Natasha, Vick and I sat by the poolside, watching people relishing the lavish buffet spread. I had yet to lay my hands on anything.

Reema, of course, had other ways to satisfy her appetite. She was as gregarious as she was gorgeous and she was a vision tonight in her skin-tight parrot green dress with her designer gold shoes and gold clutch. Her infectious laughter lit up any space she occupied and right at this moment, I noticed, she was lighting up the faces of two eager men who were engaged in conversation with her at the bar. One of them was inching towards her while sending some serious message in the way he made eye contact with her and the other was just laughing, rather flirtatiously, obviously hoping that he might be the luckier one. It was obvious that she was enjoying every bit of their attention. She was jaw-dropping hot and tonight she was the rockstar, who wore her biggest rocks and made the party rock with her presence.

I love Usher and his tune *OMG* but I couldn't dance as my knees were hurting because of the high heels that Reema had insisted I wear. She was determined to make me look glam, rather than just be comfortable in my smart casuals. My aching feet now asked me why I had agreed to be someone that I definitely wasn't. But then I reminded myself that the heels had helped me somewhat blend in with the crowd. As I entered the party I had realised that I was probably the healthiest of the women around me; they all were pencil-thin and fit snugly into their designer outfits. I was glad that I wasn't a part of this kind of social scene. And if I extended my stay I would most certainly end up developing an inferiority complex — my standards would never match theirs.

At this moment, most of these fashionable women held stem glasses and champagne flutes in their hands; I noticed that many of them were sloshed. I couldn't help but be amused at the desperate attempt of some of these women to project themselves as one with the crowd, even though it might give them a hammering hangover the next morning.

There was more happening in the party to keep me amused.

Russian and Czech girls in fish-net stockings danced on the tables whilst some eager men spilled rose champagne on them to make them look even hotter. As the evening wore on, the drunk men cheered while the dancers got more brazen with their moves. The music, the dancers and the energy in people throbbed and pulsated all night.

I wondered if these men would face the music later from their respective partners or had the wives simply become deaf and blind to these little indiscretions; a price to pay for surviving in this demanding high society where it was so easy to be overlooked. The wives probably knew that it was the wealth of their husbands that cushioned them, not their character.

People here, I noted, played by their own rules and were willing to bend them to achieve what they wanted. In a society, where there was no dearth of cash liquidity, this was indeed a cause of worry.

I looked at the bar, which was the busiest section of the party. Groups of people sat close together in the somewhat less conspicuous part of the bar, smoking joint and leaning clumsily onto one another, while a few were snogging; they were probably too intoxicated to care or maybe this sort of behaviour had become the norm. Sex was so open that it was no longer taboo.

Not far from where we were sitting, I noticed an acquaintance of ours in one corner of the dance floor —

somebody I remembered from my college days — necking a young girl, perhaps Russian, while his wife stood near the bar. She chose to ignore her husband either to save herself from humility or perhaps she no longer cared. Or she had accepted his behaviour as part of this social milieu, where interactions were as fake as the emotions of the people involved. She knew that she did not really stand to lose anything.

While the moon shone in disbelief, high in the opaque sky, the ground was throbbing with an energy that was salacious; where all scruples had been discarded as *old thinking* and replaced by the *modern*. The moon longed to shine its light on them but the people below didn't notice its presence.

I grew weary of the scene around me and longed to go back to my room in Reema's farmhouse.

Natasha interrupted my thoughts. 'The promiscuity of Delhi society is what I would like to write about next. I mean, what I have written so far is based on what I had heard and read about, but now I will have a first-hand account. What do you say guys? I would begin by saying... The life and times of the high and mighty in a city, where not only is the local cuisine spicy, but also the lifestyle of the people; flavoured with spices unimaginable...'

'Got the picture Natasha,' interjected Vick. 'But you know, there has to be a balanced view on everything. I've got accustomed to it all since I've become an integral part of this society. It's foreign to you since you've been absent from modern India or rather the new reality of Delhi. I have seen it grow. Some maybe abusing this new sense of freedom but not everyone is the same.' I was surprised at the defensive note in Vick's voice.

He suddenly turned pensive. 'Look at the positive side, Natasha, and discard the rest. I've had a very difficult early life, so this is great for me. My dad, till date, hasn't accepted my sexual orientation. It was my mother who accepted me and encouraged me to muster the courage to come out in the open, particularly after homosexuals created pockets in Delhi society that softened the stigma. It took one fashion designer to publicly accept his sexual orientation and it gave the rest of us the courage to change things for ourselves. There are numerous stories of how gays have fallen prey to societal pressures — one gay friend was forced into marriage, as his parents couldn't bear the thought of their son being a homosexual, so to save face they ruined their only son's life. I am sure there are many such cases that we don't even know about. My friend quietly succumbed to his parents' wishes by marrying a girl from a wealthy background, and the respective businesses merged to create a conglomerate. It was a horrifying business transaction in my mind and my friend should have had the courage to stand up for himself just as I did. Now they are unhappily married without any children.

'Back then, as a teenager, when I voiced my feelings to my father, he called me a drag queen and dragged me across our living room to lock me up in my room. Since then I have kept away from him. Just to please him I dated a couple of girls and I tried to get intimate with them. But, in the end, I told them the truth so that no one would get hurt. I've remained true to myself since.

'He still resents me as I am his only child and he had hopes of me getting married and giving him grandchildren. He still accuses me of letting him down and even today, when people have realised that homosexuality is as old as humanity, he will not budge from his beliefs. This rejection kills me on a daily basis, so I savour the fact that I get accepted in these parties, where I drown my innermost sorrows.'

Vick continued after a sigh, which both Natasha and I recognised revealed the sadness that he always kept so carefully hidden. He continued, 'Try to look for what is good. People are basically good but unfortunately have fallen prey to the herd mentality; without giving a thought to whether the people they are following are good or bad. What they do not realise is that this sense of belonging they are experiencing is very transient, much like the emotions and friendships they are making. We can only hope that someday they will see the light.'

Vick's words forced me to look at my surroundings in a new light. The depravity I was seeing around me was the result of the transition that the city has been seeing in the recent years; a change from a traditional society to one that was thoroughly influenced by Western culture. This was causing the confusion in the minds and behaviour of people; particularly affecting the moral stance on life in general. People were choosing drastically different ways to react to this change. Some were turning spiritual and others now concentrated on spa-ritual; just trying to pacify their senses.

I noticed a man in dapper outfit, walking towards me. His face looked familiar. 'Oh My God!' I exclaimed, as I finally recognised him as a friend from school. He had lost tonnes of weight and in fact now looked quite handsome.

'Rahul, just look at you! What are you doing these days?'

'Hi Zoya, I'm here with my beautiful wife, Seema, and I have kids, both teenagers now, and I'm into software. We just moved into our flat in Vasant Kunj, three bedrooms, and I just bought a Honda Civic and I'm buying a Toyota for my wife next month. We are set ya.'

That was a lot of information in one breath. I guess people felt the need to inform you of how well they were doing in life. But then he was refreshingly more decent than some of the others I had seen here. And that too happily married. So this was not an extinct species, after all.

'How about you? What brings you here? Still single and ready to mingle in London? No plans for *shaadi* number two?' He asked and I suddenly found him looking at me intently. Is he checking me out, I wondered. Or perhaps he was wondering why I had doubled in size where he had taken the effort to become half of what he once was. I momentarily gave him the benefit of the doubt as he continued to stare at me in a peculiar way.

'I'm good. It is Reema and Sandy's 25th wedding anniversary and this has brought all of us together again. And no, I have no plans of getting married again. Once was more than enough for a single lifetime! Besides, I'm happily married to my work — art,' I said quite emphatically.

'Cool! Not everyone is happily married! Anyway, I mean, look what happened to Sandy and Reema. What are they celebrating anyway? The fact that they now have separate lives? It's all a crazy farce,' responded Rahul.

I decided to quickly change the topic as I did not want the personal life of my dearest friends out in the open, for a public discussion. But then, it dawned on me that perhaps their personal lives had already been made public. Pushing these thoughts aside I said to Rahul, rather cheerfully, 'You've lost tonnes of weight and look great. Happiness really does reduce the waistline huh? Anyway, such a pleasure to see you Rahul. Stay in touch.'

'Sure! In fact, Seema is going to visit her parents in Chandigarh next week. Why don't we meet up and chill out together? You know what I mean? I mean you're single and I'll be temporarily single and look at you, you are still fit huh; in fact, really hot man.' He said winking and undressing me with his eyes. I wondered how I had thought he was decent at first glance. Then he gulped down his scotch as if to quench his thirst, or was it his hunger? His bloodshot eyes were now evidently filled with lust as he awaited a favourable response from me.

B*****d! I was fuming. Does he really think I would accept his offer? A second ago he was referring to his beautiful wife. Gosh! I'm exhausted. Is anyone happy out here? Does anyone here believe that marriage means loyalty to one's spouse? I sent a silent prayer with the hope that marriages don't become an extinct phenomenon. It appeared to me that Rahul too fell in the category of people who were chasing transient sensual pleasures.

I gathered myself and looked Rahul straight in the eye and said, 'Rahul, I am sure you are not looking for a girl like me. You are clearly seeking a one-night stand, which you will probably find with one of those Russian girls standing by this end of the bar, or our gorgeous Delhi ladies standing by that end of the bar. Go before they are all taken. As for me being hot love, you will discover how hot I can be, especially my head, if you do not immediately relieve me of your company.'

He stared sloppily into his empty glass and I added, 'Your glass is empty buddy, so go fill it up with some sense and meaning.'

I knew I had raised my voice just a notch higher than I should have but he had made me really angry.

Rahul moved away with some reluctance.

Now, my inner voice urged me to retire for the night. No way was I going to make a transition from being snappy to being happy. I had over-indulged in the most appetizing food and the most unappetising scenes around me. They were Delhi's a-b-c-d men; addicts of booze, cocaine and debauchery.

I looked out for my friends.

I noticed that Vick was engaged in a conversation with a young, comely, German guy. Reema was blithely busy with her friends; getting clicked by the media to be featured on Page 3. Natasha too seemed to be busy assimilating ideas for her next article — sensational stories on stoned and cheating spouses, the debauchery in Delhi society, the women who turned a blind eye to the indiscretions of their partners as long as they were sure they could own the latest bling in the market, the men who thought they could get away with anything... Natasha would surely have collected enough dough for her sizzling story to burn the pages of the magazine that featured it.

Natasha was keeping a keen eye on everything that was happening around her as was apparent from her question when she approached me, 'What was that all about?'

I looked at her and rolled my eyes up, 'Just a lot of unnecessary dilli-delhi-ing.'

Natasha and I were really taking a tour of Reema's world. I wondered how things would be 10 or 20 years from now.

13

According to Reema, the night was still young. But I certainly wasn't. A forty something body doesn't take Tequila and Vodka shots as well as a 25-year old does.

'We are going to Delhi's hot spot babes which is located in one of the malls in Vasant Kunj. It's non-negotiable guys, so stop yawning. Besides, we are only going for half an hour. Girls, keep your heads and heels high all night and Vick, forget about your beauty sleep tonight. I am foregoing the Prada and Gucci party that Sanjay is throwing at his farm in Rajokri, just to show you guys the most happening bars and clubs in Delhi.

'Stay with us at the farm, Vick, and I'll give you detox juice in the morning before some *pranayama* and yoga. So chill! Zoya, stop yawning. Please wake up and make-up. You can sleep when you get back to London. Here you are going to be a night owl.'

At this unearthly hour, when chilling was an effort and my make-up had faded, it was a little difficult to look bright and chirpy.

I saw Sandy at the bar chatting with another guy and Natasha, Vick and I went over. As he turned away from his acquaintance to chat with us I wondered what it was that had turned Sandy and Reema against each other. I had not seen them together at any point through the evening; was not even sure whether they had even exchanged a glance. Each of them was content in their own space. They were together despite their individual spaces and that I suppose couldn't be such a bad thing.

'Are you girls having fun? Can I get you another drink? I must say you both are looking dashing tonight. Hi Vick, how are you keeping buddy?' asked Sandy, as if he was really fond of him.

Vick knew that Sandy didn't like him but he just played along. 'All good, thanks Sandy. How are you doing?'

Before Sandy could respond, Natasha spoke out, 'Sandy, it's incredible how the party canvas has changed. It's electric with its sound and light but I would step back into the good old days anytime? They were fun though comparatively more innocent. What do you have to say?'

Natasha and Sandy were soon engrossed in a discussion. Unlike me, Natasha was great at remembering details about people she had just met; names, occupations, how many children they had, even what grade they were in and their last holiday destination. An impressive feat indeed and it had definitely kept her ahead in her career as a journalist.

As I watched Sandy respond to Natasha, I was once again reminded of the fact that Reema and he made such a striking couple; complimenting each other perfectly. I remember, in the early days of their marriage, they made heads turn whenever they walked into a party; they epitomised both bliss and beauty in a marriage. Tonight, however, it was heart-breaking to see them keep each other at arm's length. Would they be able to bridge the gap between them? More importantly, did they want to?

Their's was a fairy-tale wedding, meant to be a love story with happiness ever after. How did the script change? The resentment between them was clear but what was unclear was their reluctance to talk about what had brought this about. Now that we had met after all these years, I wondered if we friends would be able to help mend whatever had gone wrong between them.

It was after midnight but the frenzy of the party showed no signs of abating. Even though I was dead tired, I was fascinated by all the activities around me.

By 1 a.m. Bollywood tunes filled the air and the lights almost reached up to touch the open skies. The guests were dancing energetically; it was first 'Party On My Mind' followed by the latest Bollywood item numbers. Most people were intoxicated either with alcohol, joint, love or perhaps lust, in anticipation of bedding a new partner. With 'Sheila Ki Jawani', the enthusiasm reached its crescendo; the women swayed their hips and thrust their bosoms out; their ample cleavage drawing the male gaze, with many of them being undressed with lustful eyes.

And then Lady Gaga was on the dance floor, which had the guests roaring even louder, unable to contain their excitement. They cheered and called out to her while she sang 'Poker Face' followed by 'Bad Romance', 'Money Honey' and concluded by another hit, 'Just Dance'. She had been flown in especially for this party and had a flight to catch in a few hours. Reema, in the meanwhile, knew that she would have to change her plans of flying Lady Gaga over on her big day, as the idea was no longer original. She would have to replace her with someone bigger and better, and that too really fast. Even in this din, she asked Vick who the next best singer was. As I heard her discuss this with Vick I wondered how happy Sandy would be at the prospect that he would now have to shell out more money for the artist to be in Delhi at such short notice. Lady Gaga entranced her listeners for precisely 40 minutes following which she was escorted out by a bevy of bodyguards. As she left, the DJ began playing his numbers again and got everyone into the groove once again. The moon was getting ready to give way to the sun but the people below were still as enthusiastic about the party as though they had just begun.

Just as Reema told us that it was time to leave, Bollywood superstar Salman Khan engaged her in a conversation; they knew each other well. After a few minutes, a business tycoon, who we learnt later was from Mumbai, caught her by the waist to drag her to the dance floor. They danced intimately while he leered at her longingly. I was hoping that a couple of dances would exhaust her so that we could turn in for the night. I was depleted as though someone had squeezed the juice out of me whilst Natasha had a satisfied look on her face for having picked up enough goss for her next article. Natasha was working even when she was playing and merrily drinking her umpteenth glass of red wine. As for me I couldn't wait to do some productive work tomorrow (as opposed to my experience today) as I was beginning to feel intellectually depleted. As John Lennon had put it so incredibly, '*The more real you get the more unreal the world gets.*' At this point I felt like I was standing in a simulator, where everything was an illusion. I desperately needed my cosy warm bed where I could just be dead to the world.

I let out the longest yawn and just then a friend of Reema's (I didn't remember her name from when we had been introduced earlier in the evening), Esha came running to me with her Birkin bag. She first stared at my nondescript clutch, turned her nose up in disgust and said, 'Sweetie, can you hold onto my Birkin bag carefully, while I dance with my friend, though I don't know how since my new Jimmy Choo shoes, that I just bought from Milan, are killing my feet.'

Take them off and throw them in the pool, I thought. And while you're at it, throw yourself in too; to wash the layers off your face and to cleanse your mind.

But I responded to her saccharine sweet request with the same sweetness. 'Sure Sweetie. Don't worry. I'll hold onto it.' I said, while commanding my lips to stretch into a smile for her.

I was happy about one aspect of Delhi high society; I didn't need to remember names as everyone was either a sweetie, sweetheart, baby, babes, *jaanu, meri jaan,* dahling, and evidently more, depending on the personal equation between the people concerned. I was sure that this one was addressed as the rich bitch behind her back and on her face it was mostly dahling or sweetie, the endearment I had conveniently chosen.

As I watched her take to the dance floor I noticed that her poised coiffured look of early evening had given way to a sloshed appearance, with her hair flying in different directions. Not just her. I noticed that the appearance of many of the guests had transformed, but then it was three in the morning. One guy, in his fifties, big bellied with a diamond-studded Rolex watch, looked sloshed even as he ogled at me; he just swept past me only to collapse in the lawn. He too, must be tired and almost empathised with him.

Before I turned around to find a seat for myself, my eyes travelled to a couple sitting further away in the lawns. The silhouette of the man was all too familiar, and although vague from a distance, was once home to me.

Natasha sat beside me, telling me in mock amusement about an illustrious industrialist, in his late fifties, who had bluntly asked her if she would like to sleep with him. He offered to book a suite in the Leela for utmost luxury and lasting love-making. He promised her that she would not regret it as he was rocking in bed. She chuckled as she told me this, adding that he had probably just taken a double dose of Viagra and didn't know where to shove himself. Another man had hit on her stating that she is a sexy hot babe. She insisted that she needed cooling down and that the heat in the party was overwhelming. I took a spoonful from the bowl of ice cream in her hand and it was refreshing and reviving.

I wanted more and I did not have to wait long; my senses were soon feasting on something more alluring and attractive.

14

Rohit had always been an attractive man but I just didn't pay much heed back then. My mind had had more serious issues to deal with during that phase of my life. I had acknowledged his allure once but we both had moved on.

The sight of him now took me back into that time and space when he was ready to talk to me, to advise me whenever I need his help; to enable me to change the course of my life.

Now my heart did the perfect somersault as I watched him walk towards me. He was still as fine looking, as he was years ago. His hair had greyed at his temples and this gave an additional edge to his already good looks. There was not a single line on his chiselled face. I admitted to myself that he looked younger than I did.

'Hello Zoya, long time. How have you been?'

Every word was uttered as he gazed straight into my eyes... I could feel my heart skip a beat.

'You are looking great. I can't believe I'm seeing you here after all these years. As you know, I tried to stay in touch, but you seemed somewhat occupied. Anyway, you do look great,' he said again.

Stop being so polite. I wanted to reproach him. Unhappiness had found a way around my midriff a long time ago and even though the sadness had left me, the fat had decided to stay on. All this while I was not bothered about my weight, but since I landed in Delhi I had become self-conscious and now, standing before him, I felt grossly overweight. I promised myself that I would seek the advice of a dietician as soon as I returned to my London home.

'Great to see you Rohit. You look more than great. I see you are married to that gorgeous looking woman. Congrats,' I said while nervously turning my gaze to the attractive woman now sitting alone by the lawn.

As I spoke to Rohit, I wondered if he had changed in these intervening years. I had always found it easy to talk to him. Would I be able to interact with him in the same way? I wondered if Rohit, like me, disapproved of the vulgar display of wealth and everything else that I had been seeing around me since my arrival. And was he also cheating on his wife? Even if he was, I mused, he would surely not be making a huge show of it, like most of the people here. As I remember him, he was a very private person; that is unless the fast evolving Delhi air had got to him too.

'That's my cousin from the states; New York. She doesn't know anyone here so I was spending time with her. She's visiting after five years; recently divorced and very depressed, I'm afraid. How long are you here? Can we meet for a meal or a coffee sometime? It's been too long and I would love to take you out. You know that, don't you Zoya?' confirmed Rohit.

Charm, charm, charm. And yet there was something very real about him. I knew instinctively that he was better than most.

'Umm! Actually, I would love to Rohit, though I now have few days left. We are leaving for Goa this Friday and then I depart for London next Friday. It's kind of tight but...' I said, throwing the ball in his court, as I didn't want to let go of this opportunity.

My heart began racing as I tried to figure out what was going on in his mind. Neither of us was signing up for a one-night stand, nor a fling. Not with our history. In fact, I didn't want to appear too eager, even though I was weak in the knees just talking to him. He was just too good to fall for someone like me. Why should he? The Delhi women were too hot and sizzling for him to choose me. I was a Plain Jane — friendship material — but I suppose that was as good as it was going to get for me.

We exchanged numbers, a warm handshake and a warmer embrace before he went back to his cousin. My little heart did a happy jig as I recollected that all the while he was talking to me, his eyes had never left mine.

I was very much in love with him back then, but I never let my feeling be known to him; barely acknowledging it even to myself. And I must admit that as I was planning my trip to Delhi I had this little hope that I would run into him somewhere. After so many years, it would have been awkward to pick up the phone and call him. The fact that the pit of my stomach caved in at the mere sight of him today indicated that the love or attraction was still there.

Rohit had been my confidante throughout, as my marriage was breaking up; lending me his ear and shoulder to cry on when I discovered that my then husband was in a relationship with my cousin sister. Rohit had taken me under his emotional and financial wing, guiding me as I made the decision to end my marriage immediately. He had even ensured that I make a smooth transition to London, as I desperately wanted to make a clean start. He was like a rock beside me.

'They don't make men this sincere anymore, you know that, don't you?' said a voice close to my ear.

'Whaaaat?' I was snapped out of my reverie and found myself trying to catch my breath; to get it back into the regular rhythm.

I had not realised that Vick had come to stand beside me, where Rohit had stood moments ago.

I had been resistant to finding love again. I had made this pledge to myself, soon after my divorce, that love and commitment wasn't worth the pain. And I had cemented my decision to remain single by drowning myself in work. I, at times, regretted this stance, but my desire to educate myself on art and my ability to sell it, took over.

Natasha came over to where we stood. 'I wouldn't let him go if I were you.'

My friends were encouraging me to do what I feared the most; to allow myself to fall in love.

Was I really ready for this?

15

We were all parked at the same spot near the pool where we had our morning hot drinks; Natasha with her coffee, I, sipping on my *masala* tea and Reema and her warm water with lemon.

'What are you reading with so much concentration?' asked Natasha, while cutting a shiny red apple as she sipped on her black coffee. Strange combination I thought, but then we all have our idiosyncrasies. She was relishing every bite and sip simultaneously.

'The f*****g crime in Delhi babes. It's horrendous. Two incidents of women raped in the early hours of the morning. I thought things had changed for the better after the Nirbhaya incident in December 2012; with more security measures throughout the city.

'These monsters ought to be hanged in public after being brutally beaten. It's just not safe for women to be out on their own and if they are not raped then they fall prey to eve teasers. All this stems from an appalling upbringing; a patriarchal attitude that sees women as sex objects. Foreign media too is writing about this and Delhi is often cited as the rape capital of the world. We Delhi-ites ought to be ashamed of ourselves... I'm so glad I don't have daughters.

'As if that is not enough, a son killed his father for his inheritance and a young, newly-married man shot his bride after being married to her for a month; that too was related to money. The newspapers are nothing but depressing. I read it and then I feel low for days,' said Reema, as she let out a deep sigh.

Natasha gave a journalist's perspective, 'The shooting and the rest of the crimes are a symptom of a larger problem; the many social ills of modern Delhi — breakdown of family ties, increasing isolation and depression, fragmented family values and a wafer-thin layer of security in a marriage that filters through to the children. Then there is greed; the ravaging desire that drives people to commit all sorts of heinous crimes.

'Also babes, owing to increasing economic and emotional insecurities people have begun to act on their darkest impulses.'

But for me the greater insecurity that the people in the ever-evolving city of Delhi were facing was the fear of losing stature, so there was a mad scramble to stay right on top of things and to flaunt whatever one felt was a matter of pride; wealth, body, spouse or a fashion sense. Last night's bash was the perfect example of this mindset; people were willing to do just about anything to stay on top.

And I did not hesitate to voice this.

Natasha agreed with me, adding that the culture she left behind and the values she still upheld, no matter which part of the globe she now resided in, were absent from Delhi now.

The city today had become something she could not identify with. She had accumulated knowledge and information for her future write-ups but the issues engaged her emotions too. She voiced quite vociferously that Delhi was injured and bleeding and someone had to dress the wounds before it collapsed. She was already feeling the Delhi blues.

'Drugs being sold openly and people throwing themselves at each other, like your friend Esha and that pot-bellied man who invited Natasha to his bed; complete depravity,' I added.

'Guys, a high society party cannot be complete without mood-enhancers, okay? It's really no great shakes. No one is being forced to take it,' retorted Reema, and added, 'As for Esha... She is an ambitious woman who was dating a guy in our batch. He drove a Toyota in those days. Then a proposal came from an illustrious industrialist who drove a Rolls Royce. She dumped the Toyota and married the Rolls Royce. The woman knows what she wants.

'Besides, she has better morals than Vikas? Remember the guy who dragged me onto the dance floor? He uses his hot wife to get big business deals. She sleeps with whoever her husband tells her to and all this even though he is obnoxiously wealthy. Now tell me what's worse? I don't judge Esha since she is a today's woman, surviving in a society that is totally obsessed with youth, beauty and money; so she is definitely in her marriage to stay ahead in society. She does not hide the fact that money is important for her and in this way she is better than those who project themselves as something they are not. I too, have taken tips from her. She's the best game

changer and she is fair and lovely, just the way Delhi likes it.'
Reema smiled as she said, almost as though she was confident
that she had exonerated herself and all that we had found
unpalatable last night.

'Wow! So your friend Esha is happily married to her
husband's bank account, but as far the drugs go, are you
saying it's fine for the host to be offering cocaine, hash and
ecstasy to his guests?' I questioned.

'Grow up, babes! They are just offering it and anyone can
say no. We are adults, right? Besides, it's a matter of status
for the host to offer a choice of drugs, like they offer a choice
in alcohol. It happens in every major city, at a high society
party. It's just that it's kept under wraps, but it happens
babes, so open your eyes to the reality, however stark it may
be,' said Reema.

'I don't agree with you, Reema. Why offer something
that is detrimental to health and well-being? It is no wonder
that parents who indulge in these things are willing to
overlook when their children are indulging in the same vices.
Remember the teenagers at the club yesterday? It didn't seem
like they were in their senses. So something that begins as a
sign of status in a small party becomes the much abused norm
of a larger society.'

Natasha obviously felt strongly about the issue of teenagers
and drugs. As a journalist she was privy to a much darker side
of this menace, that we common people had no idea about.

Reema pointed out, 'The kids at the clubs were probably
just having weed guys. It's the rave parties that I'm wary

about and I've strictly barred Varun from going to any of them. They are primarily organised by elite children who have access to various drugs and they network through text messages to meet up at certain farmhouses. Now, that is not acceptable to me. Varun lets me know his whereabouts all the time guys, so I have no worries and my cute cuddly Arun is only addicted to spending time with his Cleo. My kids are clean and they are my only concern.'

'Good that you've kept Varun under your wing, love. You have the added advantage that you live in a joint family, so even the grandparents can keep an eye on the kids,' I commented, even though I wasn't too sure about its veracity.

'Yeah, it's a big bad world out here hun. We need to protect the young. They are the future of this world after all. What they do today will determine their world tomorrow. They need to be setting goals about the emotional, financial, physical and spiritual aspects of their life. You know what I mean?' asked Natasha.

'My Varun is so simple, considering our financial status. He is not at all spoilt and his only desire is to get to the university of his choice in the States. I'm so blessed babes that he is as level-headed as he is smart,' said Reema assuredly, and then continued, 'Esha has just sent her daughter, who is all of 12, to Queen Anne's school in London. She'll do her GCSE syllabus there. It has become a common practice for high-profile parents to send their kids to boarding schools abroad. It's the only way to protect them from the growing ills of Delhi society.

'As for us babes, drugs are a part and parcel of the high society bashes. We are adults and we either choose to succumb and sniff or remain smart spectators. In parties and clubs it's cool. *Sab chalta hai* babes. You know what I mean, anything goes. So just chill,' reassured Reema.

That evening we were subjected to another round of booze and bling and when we finally crashed for the day, Natasha and I told each other that we would have to take it easy the next day.

16

Natasha had been preoccupied with writing her articles all morning. She rose early to enjoy her coffee against the idyllic setting of the farm. The humidity had fallen but the heat in Natasha's head was definitely rising.

'I'm sorry but I don't agree with this *sab chalta hai* — anything goes — attitude. It's ridiculous. I'm really worried about the future generations,' Natasha said quite vociferously.

Things were not as bad as she was making it out to be, I tried to point out, mainly to quell her anger.

'Really Zoya! If you and I had kids and if they succumbed to substance abuse what would your reaction be? *Sab chalta hai*? Really Zoya? Is that all you would say to yourself to justify the social evils that have come in with the changing times. We lead by example because kids emulate our every move. Get it?' argued Natasha with a tone that was a notch higher than usual.

'Hey! You're heating up for nothing. We are not the ones running the show here. You are talking about some very influential people who rule the roost of every evolving society; they make their own rules. Unfortunately, the filth also almost always come from the top. You can write all the articles you want but will that result in action to change things?'

'Then what is the f*****g solution because what I saw in that party, and then in the night-club thereafter, is not something I would like to share with my grandchildren during my story-telling moments with them. It is besides the point that I do not want kids or grandkids, but I do have nephews and nieces and I don't want them to remain ignorant about the culture we once valued and held sacred,' said Natasha.

'You are being a tad too dramatic now, my love. It is only through collective awakening and strength of character that this collective decadence can be reversed. But I personally don't see that happening anytime soon,' I reasoned.

'Zoya, you can give me a better answer than that. Your solution is far too idealistic. Give me a real, tangible solution. There has to be a way out of this,' argued Natasha.

'All I can say is that children need to be educated on all that really matters; it's about bringing awareness amongst children who are approaching adulthood about the implications of substance abuse, multiple sexual partners and other forbidden fruits. In addition they need to be taught how to balance their lives and not just strive for material gains; personal and spiritual growth is equally imperative. It's not about more and more; sometimes less is more — the less you desire, the more peace of mind you will have. The less you get into social competition, the more time you will have for family and your true friends. Pursuing personal goals that involve creativity is equally important to one's well-being and peace of mind. Unfortunately, this has become redundant in this endless search for excess. I can only hope that each kid learns to pace his or her life, not race through it.'

I knew that the solutions I had suggested just now were too simplistic.

'Peace of mind! That's it! Health and peace of mind are under-valued. No one cares about these anymore. I finally have some clarity of thought,' said Natasha, looking reasonably pleased.

Natasha was to go back to tapping on the keyboards of her laptop when we noticed Reema approaching us. She had a radiant smile on her face.

'Had a great yoga class and I tried meditation. Man! Too many things happening inside my head. I sat for precisely two minutes 36 seconds,' she said laughing, and added, 'All I was thinking about were the things I wanted to buy; so instead of connecting with God, I made a massive shopping list. The latest Chanel bag is on the top of my list of desires. What have you guys been up to? You are up early today Natasha.'

'Yup! I had some serious work to do. As of now we were trying to find solutions to the growing social crises. Would you like to give me your inputs on the changing but corrupt times of Delhi, honey?' mocked Natasha.

'Don't be such a spoilsport Natasha,' Reema snapped back, 'You haven't come here to tear Delhi apart and neither are you here to work, so please let's have some fun. Besides babes, have you forgotten that you were a rebel back in the '80s; running away to Paris and then to New York? You now come back and try and tear down the walls of Delhi's modern society? What are you talking about? Aren't you a wee bit confused?'

'Modern... So debauchery is synonymous with being modern, is it? Aha! I had no idea. Sorry Reema, you are right. Let's all embrace modern Delhi by getting cocaine and ecstasy to the farm, a few willing men for an orgy and the best liquour that money can buy and lose ourselves in hedonistic pleasures. Let's allow it to screw our minds up completely so that we can feel *modern*,' yelled Natasha.

I froze in my chair at the heated exchange and Reema just ignored her outburst and started texting. Was it Amit, I wondered.

God have mercy on this moment because I could sense that Natasha was just about to explode. She realised that Reema had decided to ignore her taunts.

I have to diffuse this right now, I told myself.

I jumped to my feet, 'Let's go and have lunch at the Emporio Mall. We can go window shopping afterwards, have frozen yogurt from Cocoberry in the adjacent mall — or coffee and cinnabons. Which mall is that?' I asked, rambling aloud so that my voice could drown the angry voices in their heads.

'DLF Promenade. We are going for lunch to Smokehouse Deli where we can sit outside and enjoy the view of the fountain. I already have it planned. We'll have dinner next week at Emporio once we return from Goa,' responded Reema in a determined tone; she clearly did not want to disturb her carefully planned *fun* timetable.

Natasha, on the other hand, was clearly not interested in participating in today's activities — whatever they may be; one, because her creative juices were flowing and she was interested in writing her stories of Delhi and two, because she wasn't in the mood for small talk with Reema, after their minor altercation. She was clearly disappointed with Reema and her attitude towards life. Maybe she had started sensing that Reema too had changed along with the changing canvas of Delhi. She had decided to embrace everything that she saw was typical of the society that she interacted in, because she wanted to blend in. I too had been sensing this about our old friend Reema, but unlike Natasha, I was less vocal about what I liked or disliked.

Natasha added, 'Just want to say Reema that when a disease is diagnosed, a cure must be found before it spreads and destroys the entire being; in this case the core of the city of Delhi.' She clearly was determined to make her point.

She looked at Reema and I could sense sadness in her tone, despite the anger in her voice earlier, and said, 'I can't govern your thinking but I do hope, as one of your closest friends, that you will wake up from your social stupor...'

Just then we were distracted by the sound of the revving of an engine and the sound soon drowned every other sound in its vicinity, especially our voices.

Reema casually turned towards me and said, 'That is ego at its loud and lurid best. That's Sandy, of course, taking out his Ferrari...'

17

Vick, Natasha and I left early for the art show at Golf Links.

I don't know about the others but I couldn't wait to meet Bose Krishnamachari in person. I adored his art. His vibrant and vivacious works added colour to many British-Indian homes set against the backdrop of London's dreary and dismal skies. I was excited like a young teenager who was about to meet her heart-throb.

Once at the venue, Natasha got involved in chatting with one of the leading fashion designers of India. He was tall, bald and had a luminous glow on his face that I thought conveyed inner contentment. I overheard him asking her to meet him in his office once she returned from Goa, for a story on him; his successful career and the way the fashion industry of India has been getting international recognition. Natasha looked happy at the prospect of another worthwhile story on this trip. She had been amassing material for several articles; the reasons that also made her trip rewarding.

Vick looked radiant in his Indian attire with a shawl draped around him. He was a regular in these art shows and knew several established and upcoming artists. I noticed that he was busy talking to his designer friends, many of who regularly held art shows in this venue. As in the previous evening, photographers were busy here, clicking artists and their guests — art students, aspiring artists, expatriates, a few fashionistas and even fewer socialites and business people — who comprised the aesthetic sensibility of Delhi. The only time I noticed some frenzy was when Bollywood actor, Shah Rukh Khan dropped by. His presence further enhanced the colourful canvas of the art show.

I must be the happiest here tonight, I told myself as I conversed with Bose Krishnamachari. I had booked two of his forthcoming works, without the need to see them first. I knew my clientele well in London and was confident about selling them immediately on their arrival. The artist was as affable as his art, with absolutely no airs. As I was chatting with him, the media came and took a shot of us too. Now I too was a celebrity. I couldn't wait to see myself in print in the days to come.

This was where I belonged. This was familiar territory for me and I did not hesitate to mingle with the guests. I stepped outside onto the candle-lit terrace adjacent to the gallery to join my friends, Natasha and Vick. White wine and gourmet snacks were being served here. The air was clear and the shimmering stars in the clear ebony sky smiled down at us.

Reema walked in an hour later, with Arun, who wanted to immediately go around the gallery. We were told that he too was an aspiring artist. He was already preparing his parents to not expect him to enter the family business in the near or distant future. As a privileged child he had a broad palette of colours to choose from and I hoped that he would be given the liberty of choosing the right ones to create the canvas of his life with more depth and meaning.

I was laughing at something that Vick had said, when my eyes fell on the entrance to the terrace. The once familiar heaviness, the feeling of defeat, that had been my companions for years, hit me like a punch in my stomach.

My ex-husband had stepped onto the terrace with my now estranged cousin sister.

My cheerful and contented present was immediately filled with the angst of the past. I felt as though I was hanging from the edge of a cliff. What was he doing here? How was I supposed to respond to this unanticipated moment? How was I to stop being so terribly self-conscious?

I admonished myself for being weakened by this unexpectedly awkward moment that brought with it several unpleasant memories in a flash.

Natasha and Vick immediately inched closer to me like a protective shield. They urged me to say *hello* to them. Natasha gave me a strong penetrating look that commanded me to take a step forward and greet them.

'This is your moment Zoya,' said Vick, and added, 'All these years you have harboured anger and resentment. We know that it is one of the reasons why you never want to come back to Delhi. All the hurt and pain needs to fade into history. This is the opportunity. Time to show that you are capable of gracefully forgiving the past and the people associated with it. It is perhaps fate that has created this moment. Remember, the noblest revenge is to forgive.'

Natasha placed her hand around my shoulder as a sign of reassurance and said, 'The only way to overcome your fears is to confront them and you know what honey, you are not who you were a decade ago. You are now a confident, independent woman. And remember that we, your friends, are 200 per cent behind you.'

Just then, Reema breezed through the door and onto the terrace alone. I later learnt that she had sent Arun home after he had viewed the art and met the artist.

'OMG! Holy Crap! What the f**k is he doing here with that slut of a cousin of yours? Don't tell me he's still banging her. She's not a patch on you. If I were you I would throw the wine in your glass on his face and then smash the glass on her head. B***h,' Reema said under her breath.

Vick immediately responded, 'Oh! For God's sake, Reema! It's over between them. Now Zoya is getting the golden opportunity to face him and forgive him, so that she can move into a healthier state of mind. We should encourage her to do the right thing rather than needlessly add fuel to the fire.'

Natasha added, 'Remember the rough transition you made from being married to becoming single again and how tough a battle you fought during the long-drawn battle for your alimony to when you decided to settle in London. Life threw you out of gear for a while but you found your feet again. Zoya, you are a winner. You have overcome all the impediments in your life, one by one.

All that remains now is the lesson of forgiveness that you need to learn and apply.'

Turning to Reema she said, 'When is she going to get an opportunity like this ever again. Get real Reema. Forgiveness will set her free.' She paused, and added ambiguously, 'In the same way as acknowledging the truth will set you free.'

Reema gave Natasha a penetrating look, 'What the heck are you talking about? Why are you picking on me? This is not about me, but about Zoya.'

Once again, she insisted that I get a full bottle of wine from the bar and spill it on his white shirt and then smash the bottle on her head.

I could sense that things were becoming uncomfortable even between my friends, what with Vick and Natasha on one side and Reema on the other.

I countered, 'But... guys, let's just go. We seriously need to get out of here. Hey Reema, where is the Aman Hotel again? Enough of art guys, it's time to party.'

'Ah! So you are admitting defeat,' said Vick. 'Ok Zoya! Let's go... then you go back to London and remember this moment when you behaved like a coward, when you could have been the better and bigger person. Take the high road Zoya, I just know you can.'

There was a hint of irritation in his otherwise kind and gentle voice.

What had been my happiest evening in Delhi had turned out to be the saddest. How transitory was every human emotion. Gosh! Somebody get me out of this doom and gloom.

I was just about to walk out of the terrace with Reema when I turned around. Vick and Natasha were still standing in the same place, now with their arms crossed — they were clearly not going to budge unless I took a stand. They both were staring at me unblinkingly.

I stared at my friends long and hard and finally made up my mind.

Squaring my shoulders and straightening my spine, I took three long breaths and inched forward towards my former husband, who was once the love of my life, and my cousin, who I had confided in about problems in my marriage. She had listened to my woes for months and then stepped in and slept with my husband.

Yes I thought she was a b***h, but then, they were still together after so many years; that in itself spoke volumes about their strong relationship and how things might have already gone beyond repair between my husband and me before she stepped in. It's only when there is wafer-thin substance in a relationship that it eventually crumbles.

For that moment, I probably thought of myself as this slender, sensuous, self-assured, independent woman and forgot about the fact that unhappiness had found permanent residency on my mid-riff.

'Hi Sanjeev! Hi Suhana! How are you both doing? Looking well. Take care and enjoy the show,' I said, smiling confidently at them.

I didn't wait for them to recover from the stunned disbelief writ large on their faces.

Phew! I did it. I was finally free. I felt liberated from the shackles of my past hurt. I wished I would meet them again a hundred times more in the next few days, just so that I could completely offload all the resentment. I felt stronger, possibly bigger and better as Vick said I would.

Natasha and Vick both patted me on the back and told me that they were proud of me for showing the courage. Reema just rolled up her eyes and thought that we were all insane. An eye for an eye was her motto but then that was Reema's disposition; she just wouldn't spare anyone who messed with her.

'If that is how the entire world behaved Reema then everyone would become blind,' Vick said, reading my thoughts, before adding, 'Now let's go clubbing since we haven't done enough of that lately. So girls tell me where's the party tonight?'

18

Amit was standing outside the nightclub awaiting the arrival of his friend. Both Reema and he didn't let on that the meeting was carefully planned, but they didn't pretend that it was a coincidence either. None of us probed further.

After exchanging a few pleasantries we moved into the dark interiors of the nightclub. The place was heaving but Reema managed to find a table just ahead of the busy bar. The music was good — mostly commercial, and I was feeling good anyway after having offloaded the years of heaviness. I had finally closed the chapter I had been reading again and again and driving myself insane.

We celebrated with two bottles of pink champagne — Veuve Clicquot. I was suddenly energised, as were my most dear friends, who had given me the strength to do the right thing.

Reema was also relaxed now and not a trace of fury could be seen on her. She and Amit were a couple, that much was evident, as they exchanged amorous glances more times than I care to remember, but of course, she still insisted that he was just a very good friend and nothing more. They even held hands under the table thinking that it would go unnoticed and their thighs were touching more than comfortably.

After a few sips of pink champagne they decided to move onto the dance floor to dance to 'Tonight's Gonna Be A Good Night' by The Black Eyed Peas. I urged Vick and Natasha to dance with me. We stayed on the dance floor for another two songs, one was David Guetta's and the other was by Bruno Mars.

I remembered that I had gone for a David Guetta concert in London, less than a month ago. That was another reason I loved living in London, as I was able to attend concerts of all the leading artists and comedians.

The nightclub had a mixed crowd of people in their thirties, forties, and then suddenly the sixties. We danced to Bollywood's 'Party On My Mind' and then the tune changed to, 'We Are Never Going To Get Back Together' by Taylor Swift, and as we were leaving to return to our seats, Sanjeev and Suhana were getting onto the dance floor. I had seen them enter the nightclub right after us, but their presence together didn't bother me now.

What an appropriate song, I mused, as I watched them. I was now genuinely more relaxed and even smiled at Sanjeev when he looked in our direction. But I noticed that they were visibly feeling awkward. Sanjeev couldn't look at me directly and Suhana too was shifty.

Someone up there had given me another chance to hold my own. Perhaps I was going to bump into them a hundred times more during the rest of my stay after all. I felt this incredible shift within me. This had to be the biggest event for me since my arrival here.

But there was more to come. It was an evening of surprises. Sandy walked in with a girl in her mid twenties, who looked like a model. As stunning as she was, she looked out of place with Sandy. Vick and Natasha too had noticed him. Reema was too busy flirting with her so-called friend, who was now standing near the bar twirling a lock of her hair playfully around his finger and gazing into her eyes.

Sandy spotted us just as we spotted him. He couldn't even look away as that would make things awkward, so he, in his usual urbane self-assuredness, greeted us all graciously. He introduced us to the young girl, whose name quickly slipped out of my mind and Natasha quickly slipped it into a designated folder in her memory, as she always does. He announced that she was an outstation client's daughter whom he was obliged to entertain.

Try explaining that to your wife, I thought. The body language was a clear giveaway even though the tongue could lie. I wanted to say out aloud, it is 11 p.m. honey pie and this girl ought to be warmly tucked in bed by her mommy and daddy, but instead, she's out playing with you.

He fumbled for a while and then asked where Reema was, who I noticed, was now holding her friend by his ass. God have mercy on us all! Would Sandy react? We certainly did not want to witness his cool demeanour slip. Sandy turned to the bartender, commanding him to serve him his usual. The girl did the same, obviously not realising that the gesture would seem unusual to us.

Sandy with his mistress and Reema busy with her toy boy... We had definitely landed ourselves in a strange situation...

Natasha and I decided to distract him by offering to dance with him on David Guetta's 'Without You.' We practically carried him to the dance floor to evade the possibility of World War III.

Vick, in the meanwhile, ran to Reema to save her ass while she was still holding onto Amit's. The young girl was left high and dry. Vick simply told Reema that we needed to leave.

But Sandy got off the dance floor unannounced, as he was concerned about his young girlfriend. Reema by then had seen Sandy. Cool as a cucumber, she casually asked Amit to leave the nightclub and then urging us to make our way towards the exit, headed to the restroom.

Good idea. Let's leave before another surprise element walks in.

When she finally emerged, it was obvious that she had done a touch-up of her make-up and hair, mussed up earlier by her toyboy's amorous advances.

Now to take Reema out, ensuring she does not see Sandy and his mistress.

But we failed!

As Reema walked passed the bar she saw Sandy again, this time with his girlfriend.

'Hey Sandy! Is she your recent lady love? There is no dearth of pretty young things in your world, is there?' she asked caustically, before turning to his companion, 'Is your sugar daddy treating you well?'

'You have no right to speak to her like that Reema. Are you drunk?' Sandy spoke out aloud, obviously not intimated by her tone.

'To hell with you both. Sandy, I've had enough! What do you think you are doing, flaunting your girlfriend in front of my friends? Anyway, you know what, I don't care anymore, because you make me sick. You have done worse. I'm going home,' said Reema and stormed out.

We followed her out of the nightclub.

On our journey back home, there was pin-drop silence in the car. Reema was lost in her thoughts and Natasha was quietly speaking to her mother on her mobile. Vick had left in his car.

As I watched the night canvas I wondered again where my beautiful and cultured Delhi had gone? It had lost its heart, much the same way as the people living in it had become heartless; pursuing things beyond the bounds of social mores which were being thoughtlessly discarded.

I had been triumphant tonight, letting go of something that had been festering within me for a decade, and setting myself free to live again with a light heart. But what I had witnessed between Sandy and Reema tonight showed that their relationship had turned into a festering liability.

It had been a night of resolution and revelation, but frankly I was quite revolted by the way it had ended.

19

What I did not know until much later was that the war of words between Reema and Sandy had not ended at the nightclub.

Natasha and I woke up in the morning to realise that Reema was not at the farm. Just when we were about to call her, Vick dropped by. He was accompanied by Varun and Arun.

As the boys retired to their rooms, Vick told us about the events of the night before.

Loud voices and violent banging of doors woke up Sandy and Reema's household, including the servants, with a jolt, at 3 a.m.

Arun sat up on his bed, looking around his dark room. It took him a little while to understand that the loud voices that he could hear were that of his parents. They were arguing again. Once again, a deep feeling of dread began to take residence at the pit of his stomach. He heard a scraping sound on his bedroom door and opened it quietly to let Cleo in. He now sat on his bed clutching Cleo in his arms. Only Cleo understood him and did not scare him with his behaviour.

Varun, on the other hand, was older and had learned to switch off from his parents' heated arguments, since they had become an intrinsic part of living in this house. He just prayed that he would score high in his SAT exams as that would take him away from this house. He had anyway being staying at his friend Micky's place frequently using his studies as an excuse. He now regretted his decision to return home to his father and grandparents tonight. He regretted being born into this family.

He envied his classmate Micky from British School; from a humble background, Micky came to school in his father's Toyota Corolla. In fact, his father dropped him every morning and his mother fetched him every afternoon in her Honda Civic. Micky spoke highly of his parents, spent his evenings conversing with them at the dining table over dinner and had a laugh with them about this and that. They even shared his goals and encouraged him all the way. His parents were his greatest cheerleaders. He had a younger sister who he spoke very fondly of. Contrary to that, Varun admitted to himself, he couldn't recall the last time his father had encouraged him on any of his achievements, big or small. The family rarely dined together and on the rare occasions they went out to restaurants there would be fireworks before the food reached their table — so there was complete loss of appetite.

He was woken out of his reverie by his mother, shouting, 'I absolutely hate you Sandy! You are a wretched husband and father; a worthless human being. I am the one who's made all the sacrifices for this family.'

Varun realised that his grandparents stood as mute witnesses to this drama. Dadi tried to intervene but was dismissed by his mother for taking her son's side. And Dadaji had chosen to only peek out of his room. Varun had often heard him talk to Dadi about how he hoped that the children would see reason.

He stepped out of the room to see that a frightened Arun now stood near Dadi, who had her arms around him. She was once again trying to talk to his mother. Arun offered to bring her dentures from her bedroom but she told him that she didn't need them.

The boys watched as their father retaliated.

'I have sharp eyes, Reema, and the first person I saw as I entered the club was you with that useless toyboy of yours. You are a shameless woman and don't deserve to be part of this family. You are an absolute embarrassment to this family. And just what kind of an impression are you making on our two boys. They will lose their respect for you. In fact, I will make sure of that. I will make shreds of your reputation.'

Not one to be bogged down by threats, Reema shouted, 'Really Sandy? I have more ammunition up my sleeve than you would like to own up to? What can you do besides threaten me? I have always been your lucky mascot and without me you are nothing. Your luck will run out the second I run out and I ain't gonna run out empty handed. I will wipe you clean.'

The war of words would have continued if not for the doorbell.

Vick walked in and took in the scene.

'I got a call from uncle. He wanted me to come and get the boys. I am taking them with me tonight, till you both start seeing some sense.'

Without getting into an argument the boys went to their respective rooms and returned in a short while with their backpacks.

Vick did not have a word to say to either Sandy and Reema, who just stood there as if they had been turned to stone. He held a hand out to each of the boys and tried to hide his surprise when even Varun, the older one, did not hesitate to hold onto his hand. He understood how disturbed the boys must be after what they had seen and heard.

He stepped out of the house with them and shut the door behind him quietly.

Later, as he settled the boys in the guest room, at his place, they told him all that had transpired before his arrival, when they had woken up to loud voices.

Vick understood that that night the Mehra family was most certainly not a picture of domestic bliss, as they tried to project to the world outside; their home and their emotions were in total disarray.

20

Natasha and I were taken aback by what Vick had to relate. How had things deteriorated so much between Reema and Sandy, each of us wondered. We were glad that Sandy's father had the presence of mind to call Vick to pick up the kids. Did they not realise that the boys may get scarred for life? Did they even care?

Reema arrived a short while later, with beautiful cupcakes baked by a friend's daughter, who ran a bakery from her house. I had yet to see such incredibly beautiful icing with exotic gold and silver sprinkles. There were edible sugar flowers, hearts, glitters and stars embellishing each cupcake.

'Yipee! I love cupcakes,' I screeched, momentarily forgetting my worries about Reema and Sandy.

'Of course you do, Zoya,' commented Reema with an indulgent smile while passing me the tray. 'I have failed in my attempts to get you onto healthy eating, so enjoy. But, I must say that you are fab, in spite of your weight issues, so just be your confident and cool self. The rest of us have to always stay tip-top in our appearance and meet the expected standards of beauty to feel confident about ourselves. In fact I envy you and today I'm going to devour the cupcake with you. I'm going to throw my diet into the bin for today and eat to my heart's content.'

At this everyone cheered her on, till she finished her first cupcake. Reema had successfully lightened the load though she definitely still carried the heaviness from last night's showdown with Sandy.

We decided that we would indulge ourselves wholeheartedly and asked for *paranthas* for breakfast, which we enjoyed with fresh home-made yogurt, while Reema consumed every fruit under the sun, refusing to continue with her bingeing. This is even as she strengthened her relationship with her mobile. In fact she had surrounded herself with every gizmo under the sun; she skillfully switched from her mobile to her iPad to her laptop where she was now busy burning CDs for the car for our Goa trip.

When I resided here I would routinely visit the Bangla Sahib Gurudwara as did Natasha, so we decided that we would begin our day with a stopover each at the Gurudwara and the Jama Masjid.

'Why babes?' groaned Reema. 'I had made plans to shop in Ambi Mall in Gurgaon today. You guys haven't seen it yet. It's huge and we would have high tea at the Leela Hotel, adjacent to it, and discuss our exquisite ensembles for my big bash. I need an exclusive diamond set to wear on the night, which I will pick up from the jewellers in the mall, who are family friends. Let's splurge guys! Sandy announced this morning that he would also be getting delivery of his new Bentley today. He's ecstatic and has agreed to buy me the new diamond set that he was kind of resisting to earlier. I don't want to let go of this opportunity guys.'

We were surprised that things had cooled down so soon after last night's war. But then again, this spoke of the quality of marriages I had been seeing around me ever since I landed in Delhi; there was no love lost between couples, where the husband is only fulfilling his role as a provider.

Reema continued, 'Do we really have to visit these religious sites? We need something more potent to tide us through life.'

I interrupted, 'Faith is like wi-fi Reema. It cannot be seen but it has the power to connect you to your inner self and bring a lot of peace, besides, right now, we all need blessings for various reasons. Please Reema, it will be fun. Tomorrow we are all flying out to Goa. I promise to go with you to buy your set, once we are back.'

Natasha was as ready as she could be as we headed towards one of the largest business and commercial centres of the city — Connaught Place. Gurudwara Bangla Sahib was situated right in the heart of the area. Like always, the aura of the place left us awe-struck and from the chatter mode we all switched to silent mode.

As we quietly removed our shoes and walked up the stairs, we were asked to wear scarves or shawls to cover our heads. Our bare feet were scorching from the heat of the marble floor. Somehow, our devotion enabled us to transcend the heat.

We sat in complete silence before the Darbar Sahib. I noticed that even Reema sat there with eyes closed. Was she trying to find a resolution to what her life had now become? I think these were moments of introspection for each one of us.

The energy of the place uplifted us without any effort from our end. We just needed to be in the moment, while a higher energy took over.

Vick spoke out later, 'You know guys, after coming to a holy place like this, you really get inspired to introspect; concentrate on what and who matter and rid yourself of the non-essentials. Spirituality puts things into perspective. Thanks for initiating this Zoya. I would love to come here more often.'

'I wouldn't...' countered Reema, 'I love my life of profusion and confusion. I seriously do and I wouldn't give it up for anything. This is clearly a one-time thing for me. Now let's go man. I need to go and buy my diamond set. Please guys.'

We all stepped out at the rear end of the Gurudwara and walked towards the large water body known as *sarovar*. We dipped our feet in the water that had many fishes swimming in it.

The sunlight was now scorching.

'Guys! Seriously let's go! You know how I feel about direct sunlight,' pleaded Reema.

Once we stepped outside, Natasha enthusiastically selected religious CDs for her mother from the shops ahead of the *darbar*.

There were children running around, trying to sell us stuff. We told them that we were not gullible foreigners.

A young boy came up to me and asked for money so that he could buy products to polish the shoes of passers-by. He was keen to set up his own humble business.

Vick handed him a few hundred rupees, reminding him that he was standing outside the Gurudwara and that he must honour his commitment of setting up his business as a shoe polisher. He told him he would be returning next week to check on him.

Natasha and I felt sad for this boy and his impoverished state and wondered aloud how Delhi was either about abundant wealth or abject poverty — two complete extremes.

I guess we would never know what the young boy did with the money but since we were standing outside a holy shrine the least we could do was allow our cynicism to dissolve and rekindle our faith in humanity.

21

The thought of travelling got us into the spirit of celebration again, but I couldn't help but wish that Sandy was going with us. He had left for Mumbai last night and probably would have joined us in Goa, if all was well between Reema and him. Sometimes being away from home and its responsibilities could bring couples closer again. In my mind I was already planning of ways in which to rekindle their love for each other, considering their big bash was just around the corner.

Reema had settled her boys with their grandparents in Westend Delhi before heading for the airport. Arun wanted to accompany her, even shed a few tears pleading his case, but she convinced him to stay back, promising a trip soon. Arun didn't say a word then; just picked up Cleo for comfort and wished her a farewell.

Natasha and I had accompanied her to the flat and I noticed the forced smile on Varun's face as she gave him a hug. Reema did not pay much heed to it, perhaps attributing this to his teen years when kids are not very demonstrative with affection, but I thought that maybe Varun had still not recovered from the showdown he had witnessed the other night. Once again I realised that such hostile episodes left an imprint on the minds and hearts of kids this age, something that Reema and Sandy obviously overlooked.

Reema was beaming with delight, 'Beautiful sexy hot babes! We are going to have the time of our lives. We are going to have a blast everyday and every night. Let's start now at the bar. We all deserve a glass of champagne. Zoya, you are not going to have tea and Natasha, no wine for you. At this moment, it's only champagne.'

'Don't you think it's too early, and besides, don't you think you are bubbly enough?' I asked with a raised eyebrow.

'I need a bubbly to make me bubblier,' laughed Reema thunderously. 'The buzzword is party and it starts here and now.'

We each had a glass of champagne at the Sports Bar at the airport once we had checked in our bags and had our boarding passes in our hands. Reema came across a well-groomed gentleman in his business suit who was on his way to Mumbai; it seemed he also knew Sandy. After they exchanged pleasantries, and we had moved on, Reema conveyed to us that he was a paedophile, but was well-connected within the power corridors of Delhi. This made the Delhi socialites invite him to their every bash — they either feared him or favoured him. His wife was aware of his sordid activities and stayed away from him for lengthy periods of time by going home to her parents in Pune. For some reason, her parents did not support her need to seek a separation, so now she kept her distance from him and was mostly seen in the spiritual circles of Delhi.

Lastly, under her breath, Reema whispered that Sandy was very close to the gentleman. We disregarded her last comment; the mind refusing to acknowledge a thought that was too frightening. She quickly distracted our minds by jovially telling us that what happens in Goa stays in Goa. She warned us about the wild times we should expect to have and therefore the need to be sworn to secrecy.

The travel time was just two hours and Natasha fell asleep while Reema and I sat together to catch up on old times.

Somehow the conversation steered to Rohit and how good a friend he had been at the time of my wedding. Reema had noticed us chatting on the evening of the art show.

Finally admitting it even to myself, I said, 'I think I fell in love with him then. We were on the phone practically every couple of hours. I was sharing every morsel of my anguish when I got to know about my husband's affair with my cousin. I gradually began to look forward to his calls. I just didn't acknowledge it to him or to myself during that very trying time of my life. I left for London almost immediately after my divorce came through and then somehow we lost touch, as I was trying to settle down to a new life, but I could never get him out of my head, you know what I mean?'

'So what are you saying?' Reema asked, 'You wanna get laid now. I mean instead of having him in your head you want him in your bed? I can call him to Goa if you like. I'll tell him we are celebrating my wedding anniversary and he has to be there. I'll send him the ticket. What do you say? Anything for you babes, it's only a ticket and imagine you could have the most rocking time with him there. I'll book you a separate room with him... Cool?'

Rolling my eyes at Reema's one-track mind I confessed, 'Listen love, I really want to meet him but not here. I was wondering if it would be ok for me to meet him alone, outside social circles I mean. I'm not looking for a fling, but a long-term friendship... perhaps not even a relationship. I mean, I don't know... but I definitely want him to be in my life in some capacity.'

Reema broke into peals of laughter and then suggested that I invite him to the farm and make out with him because there was no such thing as a platonic relationship between a man and a woman. She insisted that I have a one-night stand with him since I was leaving in a few days and I needed to get it out of my system.

If only Reema understood the value of love and friendship with the opposite sex without the sex. She mentioned that there were sex education classes for married and single people in Delhi that I could attend.

'Zoya, you look like you could do with some hot moves. Get out of your shell woman. This is modern Delhi; live your life on your own terms without any inhibitions. Embrace this spirit and you will be very happy.'

Was it because of the increasing amount of failed marriages in Delhi that people here would rather have casual sex with multiple partners than commit time and energy to one committed relationship? Was it the fear of getting hurt? Or was it that life was moving at such lightening speed that no one had the time and patience to work on their relationships. They would rather appease their carnal desires. If it didn't work it would be thrown away and replaced with another.

Most people either went into a sleep mode if their relationships didn't work or some shut down completely, while others, who perhaps had the time and means, would restart with a different partner. It was all about delete but never about save.

But I was definitely disposed to giving friendship a chance. Reema had perhaps ceased to believe in enduring relationships so she viewed men as a piece of meat to be used and disposed off.

Natasha had heard the tail end of our conversation and commented how frivolous Reema had become. Modern Delhi had turned her into a person who knew the price of everything but the value of nothing.

'Babes, I do believe in love and intimacy, trust me I do, but just not with my spouse. I was smitten with him to begin with, until I was bitten. But that's a long story and will unravel when the time is right. The truth is that he is the one who taught me that love is about money,' Reema said in her defence.

22

Here we were again sitting by the poolside, this time it was at the Lemon Tree Hotel, Goa. Vick was expected to join us tonight before dinner.

We sipped on our cocktails as we planned lunch at Calangute, since Natasha wanted to be in a populated beach and Reema didn't mind, since she could feast her eyes on all the hot men.

'Hey babes, we are heading towards the *Queen of Beaches* now,' said Reema. She chuckled and added, 'The weather is bliss; no rain so far but we are going to get wet anyway ogling at all the hot men on the beach.'

She was, as usual, on her mobile, chatting with Amit. Natasha and I knew it the moment she said *hello*, as her tone and body language changed. No matter what mood she would be in before the call, she would be radiating joy afterwards. Her need to reassure him that she wouldn't be ogling at other men was another telltale sign that this was much more than mere friendship, besides addressing him as *jaan*. But there was no point in questioning her about it as we knew that she would deny it completely.

We were like giggly schoolgirls again, eating, drinking wine and feasting our giddy eyes on the men. At least mine were, as I wasn't accustomed to wine at all. The men came in all shapes and sizes. While some returned our ogling glances, three of them approached us as we sat in our bathing suits with each of us wrapped in light chiffon sarongs. They bought us a cocktail each and we chitchatted.

The beach was bursting with people even as we were bursting with exhilaration and even though we had enough to chew on, Natasha suggested that we go to Baga beach before heading for the Chocolatti in Candolim for an evening cuppa and chocolate gateau. It was her first time here so she wanted to tick off all the items on her to-do list.

I, on the other hand, had come here for my first two wedding anniversaries and had stayed at the Fort Aguada Hotel that was part of the Taj group. Our seven-day trip was both fun-filled and fulfilling as it was like reaffirming our wedding vows. In the third year we went to Verbier in Switzerland for skiing and we kissed and cuddled on the slopes like newlyweds. Our marriage went from strength to strength as we both wore happiness like a comfortable old coat that we promised never to let go of. Overnight, life's climate changed, painting a very grim picture for us and we both discarded the coat for a new one; at least he was the first to do so.

At the Baga beach, we sat in one of the shacks, sipping on exotic cocktail with the most delightful view of the Arabian Sea and enjoying the hustle bustle around us. There was a lot of activity on the beach. Among other things, we noticed athletic, shirtless hunks making tattoos on women as they lay on the sand. Reema was tempted to get a tattoo, but we discouraged her. I secretly wondered if it was Amit's name she wanted tattooed on her hip.

Reema finally announced to us, 'Guys, I have a headache. Why don't you carry on here till sunset; click some pictures, put them on Facebook and meet me back at the hotel by 7 p.m. I'll pop a pill and rest before your return and then we settle for a plush experience tonight at the Thalassa restaurant which serves Grecian food or we head for the Anand Bar for a more local, earthy experience. It's a shack, right in the middle of open fields and it serves great Goan food. It is rustic and yet romantic. We can call those guys who had bought us drinks earlier, to add to the ambience.' She added after looking at our surprised expressions, 'I had taken down their numbers. We'll decide in the evening what we settle for and I'll inform Vick so he can meet us there directly. Cool?'

'Cool love, but we'll leave with you if you're under the weather. We can be in the sun tomorrow; we still have a few days. Come Natasha, let's go. We can even call a doc if you need one,' I suggested as I abruptly got up.

'No babes! It is Natasha's first time here, so chill. I'm a big girl. I'll take a cab and head straight to the hotel; no big deal. I'll speak to the boys on the way. Varun just texted me and I'll check on the little one since he was so weepy when I left him,' insisted Reema, before she continued, 'Tomorrow I'll be hale and hearty; ready to party all day and all night. We'll even have high-tea at the Chocolatti in Candolim which is walking distance from our hotel, so please don't go there today. Make the most of the beach. It's all under control guys. Now chill,' said Reema, emphatically, determined as usual, to have the last word.

Natasha and I soaked in the Goan air as we gazed delightedly at the sky and its changing hues; first it was golden, then beige and then saffron, followed by crimson and finally ebony. The serenity with which the sun was setting permeated our being, making us one with the experience. The gentle waves of the water sent ripples of joy inside us. We missed Reema and wished she too would experience this moment that was as soothing as it was moving.

Such moments evoked a cocktail of emotions as I particularly recalled my times here with my former husband and when I did so, I realised that we can never divorce our memories of the one we are estranged from. Natasha sensed my pensiveness and as if she read my mind, responded...

'Zoya, I learnt a long time ago that we can't alter what has happened. This incredibly striking sunset is a clear reminder of how someday the sun will set on our lives. That is the final truth and while we are here we must allow this beauty to wash over our being now, because that is the only truth; our present. Crying over the past is such a waste of precious time; which is our present. So don't do it.'

I turned to her and nodded with a smile. I was grateful for having Natasha in my life as she continued to give me good advice.

Natasha added, 'These colours of the sunset evoke passion in us Zoya and what you need to do is to pay heed to Reema's advice on allowing Goa to bring out the beast in you. My dear Zoya, Rohit is as good an idea as ordering a cocktail and toasting it to the promise of a life full of love.'

I nodded again in agreement...

23

'What the hell is going on?' I looked at Reema in horror as she tried to cover herself with her quilt. She was partially shielding her *partner in crime* with her body. Thank god for these miracles. I had no desire to see Amit in the nude.

'And what is he doing here? And didn't you say that you were going to bed because you were unwell?' asked Natasha, her face reflecting horror and disgust.

'I'm sure her headache has eased now... or whatever her excuse was to leave us at the beach. No bloody wonder you needed a separate room for privacy, and no wonder Sandy and you aren't getting along. It is because you are too busy with Amit.' I realised that I was now yelling at her.

'We've been sitting watching the sun go down while you idiots have been going down on each other,' Natasha yelled.

Both Natasha and I had sensed that something was going on between these two; the amorous glances and the roving hands had said it all. But to actually catch the two in the act was a lot to digest. What was going on with Sandy and Reema? Reema definitely was not a woman in love with her husband and Sandy, as we had seen him in the company of his so-called client's daughter, was not a devoted husband either. And if things had really fallen apart like this for the two then what was all this excitement about an anniversary party?

'Natasha! Zoya! Let's talk tomorrow,' Reema said calmly, before adding, 'I can't explain myself to you like this. And neither of you have the right to judge me or my non-existent marriage.'

Reema's nonchalance was disturbing, as though getting caught was normal for her and sleeping with a man younger than her was even more normal.

Ignoring her words I turned to Amit, trying to avert my eyes from all that was on display. 'Excuse me Mr. Hot-Ass and Six-Pack, would you mind covering them both, as well as your other body parts and getting out of our hair? We need to speak to our friend?'

Unaffected by the tone, Amit just smiled, rolled up his jeans and picked up his shirt and while making his exit blew Reema a kiss, saying, 'Baby you are hot!'

She looked back at him with undisguised adoration to return the compliment, 'You too babes!'

She too wore her clothes, completely blasé about our presence in the room, and calmly turned towards us with a satisfied look, 'Man… I love them young… they are most feisty in bed.'

Natasha and I sat on the edge of her bed with unmasked disappointment and annoyance, as Reema settled back against the large pillows.

'Seriously girls… I am having the most amazing time. A woman has a right to be happy.' She giggled before adding, 'I have no regrets for enjoying the ride with him. He satisfies me sexually and more importantly, he makes me laugh… and I am happy.

'We have an indefinable chemistry between us and I am not going to apologise for it. I take my commitments very seriously guys. I'm not going to flagellate myself for thoroughly enjoying the company of a man who appeared at my doorstep just when I needed to be rescued from my empty marriage. I mean, am I not allowed to, just because of the little technicality of my life, like a marriage! I don't get it! Are you guys going to clip my wings?' asked Reema frowning, looking at Natasha and me intently.

'You know Zoya, don't mind me saying this, but you're single and yet you tend to be too strict with yourself. After your break-up you should be living happily with any and every man. But you just don't know how to chill. I'm not like you babes. I need to be in love. I need attention. I am all knotted up inside and Amit unknots me. I am so restless without him and he has the ability to set me free from myself. He is just a-m-a-z-i-n-g and a g-r-e-a-t lover. Come on guys stop judging me.'

I'm not a saint either, Reema dahling, I said to her in my head, but then if I was married I would think twice and then maybe, maybe not.

Gosh! The Delhi air was rubbing onto me. My darkest impulses were surfacing — in the same way as an almost animal desire had taken over the lives of most people here.

'Now, I have a headache,' said Natasha, breaking into my thoughts. 'This is definitely not how I had imagined our Goa holiday. Do you have anything for a headache Reema? Sorry, you obviously didn't need a headache pill. Would you have one Zoya…'

Reema interrupted, 'Guys, we can either sit and talk about this or just put it aside and enjoy some great Grecian food. Vick is meeting us at Thalassa in an hour, so can we please move on from this space? Natasha, get your skates on babes! Let's just be happy. I wanted to invite Amit for dinner, but you guys will make it too awkward for him. That is not fair but I'll compromise by not inviting him. Friends are meant to be saving each other's asses but you would most willingly kick mine.' She laughed out aloud as she said this.

Her laughter seemed to lighten the mood. In all fairness, we hadn't flown all the way to Goa to get on her case. So Natasha and I both took a deep breath and decided to terminate this conversation. In any case, it seemed as though Reema had developed a thick skin about this, so there was no point trying to get through to her. So we backed off that instant.

Natasha and I quietly left her room to return to our room — adjacent to hers. The sound of her moaning had prompted us to barge into her room, flabbergasted. We thought that her headache must have escalated into a terrible migraine. We didn't know that the sound was all about pleasure and not pain.

At this moment, my thoughts were a jumbled mess of anxiety and apprehension. This is because Natasha and I had rung up Sandy in Mumbai and had convinced him to come to Goa to surprise Reema.

What was going to happen now?

I needed a food rush to get me out of my present mood and knew that Natasha would go for her customary red wine.

Maybe we both needed to hit the bottle tonight.

24

At the Vagator beach in North Goa was situated a slice of heaven and that was our restaurant.

Reema had chosen well.

Thalassa means *From the Sea* in Greek and the view of the beach and the Arabian Sea from the restaurant were breathtaking. The beach was sufficiently lit by the moonlight for us to take in the sight and sound of the waves and the air was clear and calm. The restaurant did not have ostentatious décor; probably to make the most of the natural beauty of the beach and sea. The white walls around us, with open-air seating, made it easier for us to soak it all in. It truly surpassed our expectations and we were all happy to be together again despite the drama a few hours ago. The sea breeze blew away our anger and we were determined not to bring it up again over this blissful dinner.

Vick looked striking in his Nehru-collared burgundy shirt. He was fair with a very clear complexion and he looked dashing in dark colours. Reema, Natasha and I wore long floral dresses that were apt for a vacation and location like this; summery and sensuous.

Natasha and I had spent a lot of energy confronting Reema so we decided to replenish it by ordering some appetisers soon after we had settled down. Vick and Reema were happy, as always, to satisfy their appetites by taking in the ambience of the place. They both lived on love and fresh air and considered eating anything but organic, unfashionable.

Tzatziki with pita bread, few Grecian salads and hummus, melted cheese on pita and a tuna dip did the trick. Natasha was looking happier and her expression, I knew, mirrored mine — a satisfied look. I told myself that since there was no love or lovemaking in our lives, food was a great substitute satisfying all types of hunger.

We both giggled as we observed Vick and Reema peck on their individual plates of salad. They had both engaged themselves in the finer details of the restaurant and Vick voiced his desire to open one of his own. One of his friends had just opened his own place, The Blue Door Café, at Khan Market and he was inspired to do the same.

'My ultimate dream is to own a restaurant at Khan Market. I would serve only high quality organic dishes. I'm vegetarian, so no meat; green and lean cuisine — the way we like it Reema.'

'You could name it Green Light,' suggested Reema, who was once again sprightly, as though no turbulence had taken place a short while ago. But then that was her and we loved her; for better or for worse.

Reema added, 'But vegetarian won't bring the bacon home. If you want to make money then non-vegetarian and liquour license is a must. Sandy could help you with that as he knows all the ministers.'

Natasha and I decided to order the main course. Looking at the menu together we whispered to each other how we would break the news of Sandy's arrival to Reema. We knew that Reema would cut us both in half, just as deftly as she was cutting the bread roll.

Reema asked suddenly, 'What are you guys whispering about? You haven't given any inputs on Vick's aspiration of opening a restaurant? I thought you were both quite enterprising, what happened?'

We decided that now was as good a time as any.

'Reema,' Natasha began cautiously, 'You know we mean well for you, right? I mean you know that in the depths of your being, right? We only wish you well because we genuinely love you.'

'Get to the point guys. What's with all this sugar-coating?' Vick asked, looking at us very suspiciously.

Reema too stared at us with a piercing gaze before asking, 'Just spill it out. What is it?'

Reema listened in silence as we broke the news of Sandy's imminent arrival the next morning. But the calm countenance turned into distress and we watched the frown deepen on her forehead. She was looking at us as though we were her greatest enemies.

Vick broke the silence.

'So that's great news Reema. I mean he may not think the world of me but it will be great to have him around. He is your husband and this celebration is all related to your 25th wedding anniversary. Well done Zoya and Natasha for taking the initiative. You did a great thing, so why on earth are you both looking as if the world has just been torn apart?'

'Because Vick, that is just what is going to happen. I don't think it's such a grand idea. Sandy coming here will be a grand fiasco. I am not alone here, Vick. I'm here with a man,' confessed Reema.

25

We headed to the Ashwem beach, to the Shanti Goa Lounge and restaurant. The place was known to serve the best Martinis and Natasha wanted to try some — another item on her to-do list, particularly since we didn't know how earth-shattering the next morning would be. If the world ended tomorrow, with both Reema and Sandy drawing out their daggers, then there would be no more Goa for us.

The place had a great ambience. As we entered, we met our common friend, Vikas, from Delhi, who was taking a break with a couple of his guy friends. They were sitting near the bar drinking along with a few young women, who Reema pointed out were all escorts; either Russian or Czech. They were all smoking pot. They were as stunning as they were stoned. Vick raised an eyebrow as he knew all the men and stated that each one of them was married. Obviously that little fact was not a deterrent to them enjoying this hedonistic holiday. Natasha thanked her stars for never having got married and I too wanted to celebrate my single status.

'I just don't think commitment holds the same meaning as it once did when my mom and dad were married. It's not that I don't believe in love but I think marriages today have become complicated and eventually it is just the convenience of the set-up that keeps couples together,' I pointed out.

Vick with his usual good humour added, 'I guess commitment now means I love you till the next one comes along; to hold and to cherish till the next man or woman do us apart. Having said so, I would still want to fall in love and get married; perhaps in London.'

The conversation seemed to have a strange effect on Reema.

'Breaking news on my love life, guys!' she announced, loud enough for the guests at the tables close by, and continued, 'I asked my boyfriend, Amit, to meet me here and I f****d his brains out this afternoon and then was caught red-handed by two of my best friends. To add fuel to the already hot fire they have decided to invite my husband, who I have not bedded for the past two and a half years, for reasons which all of you must hear now, since it's time to lift the veil.'

The three of us were stunned by her words. While Natasha and I were wondering how to react to this, Vick spoke up, 'Reema, you don't owe us an explanation. We love you all the same and will support you whenever you need it. What's the big deal? I mean everyone has a right to be happy nah? Let's just celebrate tonight and drink to friendship and reunions.'

Reema gave him a sharp look of disapproval for interjecting and said, icily, 'Let me talk Vick and I don't want anyone to intervene while I speak.'

My heart skipped a beat. Natasha too was looking visibly uncomfortable. We didn't know what lay ahead. The expression she wore at that moment foretold a tornado coming our way. Her body language could be likened to that of a warrior who was preparing for war, hard and hostile.

Vick appeared calm, but then he always was. He always had a balanced view of everything. He turned towards Reema, giving her his complete attention, with his eyes fixed on hers.

'Go on Reema,' he encouraged.

'There has been a big hole in Sandy and my marriage, for a few years now. He has been bruising me emotionally. To the world, he is a cultured man. People actually are taken in by his charm. But I know another side of him that is manipulative and mean. For many years, after our wedding, I devoted my life to his dream of becoming a big man, with a certain position in Delhi society. He would do anything for recognition, often resort to unscrupulous ways. Not happy with just acquiring wealth, he wanted to reach a certain position of power, where he could manipulate and control for his own benefit. I supported him all the way. I watched him as he fought his own brother, too, dragging him to the courts to get the lion's share of their assets. Did you know that his brother died under mysterious circumstances? No one knows the truth, as all evidence was buried rather quickly.

'I have also seen wealth and popularity before I married Sandy. You should hear the scandals and scams he has been involved in — tax-evasions and money laundering, with the Directorate of Revenue Intelligence swooping over our lives every other day; that is even as Sandy went into hiding. I would be there covering for him and supporting him in whichever way I could. He convinced me that whatever he was doing was in the best interest of the children, even though he barely had time for us. The neglect deepened and each time he would be with us he would be abusive and edgy. When I insisted that I wanted to leave him he would soften momentarily and plead with me for five more years — time for him to make it big. He insisted that his risk-taking was to ensure that we as a family could afford every luxury under the sun.

'During these times, he would be more volatile when pushed for answers, but on cooling down he would succeed in convincing me that he needed my love and support because he too loved me dearly.

'When this continued for years, I fell into deep depression and had to seek professional help. Not just that, I began taking Prozac in high doses, to the extent that I became dependent on it. Sandy would insist that I had lost my mind and this would further fuel our fights. I began to lose interest in his world and life in general. I wanted to quietly slip away but held on for the sake of my boys.'

The three of us listened in horror. Drug dependence, depression… What more was she going to reveal to us?

Reema continued, 'I then ran from pillar to post for answers; the top tarot card readers, past-life regression therapists, who charged me the earth, and others. It worked in a strange way; the more money Sandy amassed the less I began to value it. I would squander it mindlessly on every new-age psychic reader who I knew in my heart was bull-shitting me.

'And then I met somebody, who helped me heal — somebody who helped me regain confidence in myself. I admit we had a roaring affair, but then there was no love in my marriage. He was my first and others followed. This became my way to retain my sanity and survive in a marriage that was dead and buried with no chance of resurrection.

'The final straw was when I was home in Westend once and Sandy told me that he was leaving for a business trip and would be back the next day. I don't know what made me go for a drive to the farm and there I saw the bedroom light on. I caught him with two naked hookers, who were having cocaine and sex with him. There was no reaction on seeing me; perhaps he was stoned or he just didn't care... I still don't know the reason.

'As if that was not enough... the next morning there was a raid at the office, our home, and then finally at the farm, where packets of cocaine were discovered in the boot of his Rolls Royce. He asked my cousin, who was in financial distress, to take the blame in exchange for him taking care of his family. He promised him that he knew a minister who could get him out in no time, which he did only weeks later, but the trust between us had been shattered forever.

'Varun has caught onto his father's unscrupulous behaviour. Arun is too young to understand these things, but he senses that his family is far from perfect. His love for his father makes him go for golf practices with him, but Varun hides behind excuses of schoolwork. As a mother, I know that he is simply keeping a distance. I can still see the fear in

Varun's eyes each time he is confronted by his condescending father. It has become an annoying habit with him to constantly criticise Varun, which I know demoralises him and keeps him from unleashing his potential.'

Was she talking about the same Sandy that all of us admired for his polished demeanour? Had he really sunk this low? My mind flew back to the time Reema and he got married. A perfect match; that is how we friends viewed the marriage.

Reema's words brought me back to the present, 'He has stopped using the farm for his sexual indulgences. He got what he always aspired for; fame, fortune and most importantly, power. His friendships are never without an agenda.

'He has young models by his side to give him physical pleasure without any emotional fulfillment. As I see it, he is the loneliest man I know even though he revels in his fame and recognition.

'I can neither leave him nor love him, so I have learnt to capitalise on all that he has accomplished for my own comfort. He has never given a dime for my feelings or that of the children, yet he has always said that whatever he has done was for us. I know that Varun and Arun, my babies, have grown up with great insecurities. I feel sorry that I could not shield them from the ugly truths of our lives.'

We watched Reema's face as she related how things had changed for Sandy and her; she was animated and seemed to be reliving every painful episode. We understood that she needed to let out all the bottled up emotions and therefore just listened quietly, almost as though we were trying to make up for all the years when she needed our support but we weren't around for her.

Reema continued, 'Initially, when I was in the thick of clinical depression, I went to seek support from my parents, but Sandy presented himself as a fully responsible husband and father. They were also in awe of what he had achieved and were thrilled when saying, "Meet our daughter. She is the wife of Sandy Mehra" or "She lives like a queen in her palace, with a fleet of luxury cars and servants. She has two managers to manage the running of her home. She is so blessed that she travels only first class to the choicest of destinations, five times a year, with her husband and lovely children. Last year she went skiing with her children and the year before she was on the Caribbean cruise. There is not a single country that she hasn't visited. May Goddess Lakshmi continue to shower her blessings on my child!"'

My heart sank with each word that Reema uttered. Natasha too was horror-struck at the revelations. I noticed that Vick had tears in his eyes. But there was also an unspoken anger. Perhaps he would reach for Sandy's collar when he saw him next. The three of us felt so guilty for having been oblivious to the pain that Reema had gone through, believing that all the glitter in her life was pure gold.

'Then my life took another turn. I began visiting this enlightened lady who became my Guru. I told her everything about my life. She rendered me the strength that I needed to stay afloat. She completely weaned me off my anti-depressants and taught me to connect to my inner reservoir of love and knowledge. I began meditating, and by doing so, became confident to be able to live my life on my terms. I stopped going to her too, when I began to feel strong enough to stand up by myself without any crutches. So, I do believe in a higher power except that I believe that it lies within us and I do believe in the power of money more than the power of love.

'I threw out the rulebook and then I took a firm stance to live my life, by my own terms and decided that I would be happy no matter what, without any expectations. I began working on my appearance with the help of a professional image consultant and personal stylist. Then I began spending Sandy's hard-earned money, like water. And why not?

'Guys, we are all products of our circumstances. I have adapted myself to the equation of my marriage in my own way. I do not want a divorce from Sandy now because he can give me a lifestyle I have begun to enjoy. And why shouldn't I enjoy? I no longer invite unnecessary stress or strife by focusing on the negative aspects of my marriage. My only responsibility is towards my children.'

None of us could respond to what Reema had just revealed. I asked myself, what right did I have to judge Reema for the path she had chosen for herself. We just sat in silence and the air outside too seemed to have become still after hearing her story. Reema broke the silence.

'You know guys, after Sandy broke my heart I became practical. My heart became the most invulnerable part of me, and just so you know, I am not in love with Amit. I am well aware that he won't last with me. The sensuous pleasure, although transient, is all I have to hang on to and at this moment I love being with him because he makes me feel good.'

Natasha and I felt like idiots for having insisted on Sandy joining us in Goa. Now that the lid was off, and the facts had been laid bare, we wished we could turn back the clock. But now we began to question why he had agreed to fall in with our plans. Was it because he wanted to prove that he was the good guy while Reema was the one who didn't appreciate him?

There were other questions speeding through my mind. Why had Reema chosen to keep things from all three of us, considering we had been friends for years. I could appreciate that with no support system, with even her parents not understanding her plight, she must have felt so helpless at times. She could have especially reached out to Vick, who stayed in Delhi.

Vick echoed my thoughts when he finally spoke out. 'Baby, you always kept your pain under wraps even when I asked you what was wrong. Why Reema? I can't even believe that you were on anti-depressants. But the really sad part to this tragic story is that you chose to keep it from us and that makes us all just fair-weather friends.'

Natasha placed her Martini on the table and hugged Reema. She held her in her embrace like she was never going to let her go. And the two soon had tears running down their cheeks.

Natasha was the least emotional of us four and I was taken aback at her reaction.

'I also feel like I've been left out of the crucial chapters of your life. You must have been so affected by the things happening in your life that you couldn't even reach out to us. I despise Sandy for all that he put you through and my heart bleeds for you. You've picked up the pieces of your marriage. We had not been around for you to lean on then but we are here with you now,' Natasha said.

'How did Sandy transform from an angel to a devil? Or were we so taken in by the charm that we did not see the power-hungry, manipulative and corrupt individual behind it?' Natasha was talking to herself. I agreed with her.

Reema now looked her usual self. Breathing deeply, to take in the clean sea breeze, she stated how glad she was to be here with us in Goa. I marvelled at her ability to switch from one mood to another; she was her vivacious and vibrant self again.

She announced, 'Tomorrow we will leave early for Candolim and then take the taxi to Miramar beach. If you guys are looking for serenity, then we'll go to the Aguada beach for lunch.'

Then in her usual chirpy tone she announced, 'G-u-y-s I am bushed. I need to hit the pillow man.'

We echoed her sentiments and decided to turn in for the night.

Natasha and I tossed and turned in our beds, thinking about all that Reema had said. I also thought about my own life, especially about my broken marriage. I had chosen to walk out when I discovered my husband's infidelity. Reema had chosen to live through it all, and still was. I could now understand why she wanted me to react to my ex-husband and his partner with such hostility at the art show. She probably wanted to publicly humiliate Sandy, but could not do so because of the children.

I shared this with Natasha and she agreed with me.

However, even though we sympathised with what Reema had gone through, Natasha could not help but question the path Reema had chosen to find her solace. Plunging into a lifestyle bereft of a moral code just to spite the infidelities of her husband was not a path that she herself would have chosen, if faced with a similar situation in life. Instead of a meaningless existence, where she was surrounded by the shallowness of Delhi high society she could have built a more meaningful life for herself; even if it meant using Sandy's money for some altruistic purpose.

'I don't want to judge, since each of us has our own individual solutions to our problems but I do pray for Reema to respond to darkness by lighting a candle in her heart,' she said finally.

The emotional upheavals of the evening and the silence of the night soon took its toll on us and we drifted off to sleep.

26

The exotic palm trees, the vast Arabian Sea, the enchanting golden Candolim beach and the energetic breeze, all made an excellent combination and flushed our hearts with joy. The waves touched us, embraced and seduced us and captured our hearts. All four of us glowed like we had just made love; Reema most likely had, before discreetly sending her lover Amit back to Delhi. It was an intelligent decision given that Sandy could land up any time though he hadn't shared his schedule with any of us.

Vick took charge of the morning activities and booked us for parasailing. Natasha insisted on going scuba diving but for that we would need to go to the Grande Island that was just off the coast, near Vasco de Gama. Besides, that would be half a day's activity. She was fit and had done it before, whereas I would need a few lessons. Vick and Reema however did not show much enthusiasm for the sport. Reema, in particular, was a little distracted because she hadn't heard from Varun for a while. The last time he had texted was the previous evening; to inform her of his plans to stay at his friend's place. He wanted to study with him. She dismissed her worries, deciding to call both the boys once we stopped by at a restaurant. Nobody had breakfast besides our morning hot beverage as we had unanimously decided on having brunch in a restaurant at the Fort Aguada Hotel. Reema suggested, 'Let's book scuba diving for all day tomorrow, if you so desire Natasha. Zoya, you can visit the art galleries, though they may be closed with tomorrow being a Sunday. We'll enquire, but first we'll have breakfast together at the German eatery on the Baga river creek. It is pure bliss and then we'll all split; do our own thing.'

Natasha and I agreed excitedly as we both needed our me time.

Reema and Natasha shared the eagerness of young teenagers as they ran across the beach, bare feet in their swimsuits. I had opted for the more conservative one-piece swimsuit, with a floral sarong loosely wrapped around my hips, for this beach adventure. I watched as they teased the white waves and their coolness with their feet. They splashed water on each other and screamed in elation. Their euphoria tickled my senses. I was sure it must have also touched Vick.

Somehow, inspite of the bonhomie our surrounding was trying to inspire, Vick and I started talking about Reema's revelations of the night before, even as we walked the beach together.

'It's unbelievable how none of us realised the rough ride that Reema had to go through. I can't believe Sandy is so self-centred and manipulative. I've lost all my respect for him.'

'Same here. I feel like a fool for not realising what she has been going through — particularly as I reside in the same city. Have to say, she has successfully masked her problems. But then, if you look closely at the high society of Delhi, you will realise that most of them have troubled personal lives; they have really learnt the art of keeping up appearances.'

'Guys, stop chatting. This is the moment to go crazy! Come into the water,' Reema yelled from a distance.

'You don't know what you guys are missing. Run for the waves guys. How can you even think of staying away,' echoed Natasha.

We splashed, swam and shouted with joy.

We were rejuvenated once again, celebrating our friendship that had somehow become stronger overnight. We let go of the pain of our past as we exercised our lungs, by shouting out our joy.

Parasailing was quite an adventure; probably the most adventurous activity I had ever engaged in. Buoyed by the wind, and flying over the vast expanse of the sea was both thrilling and frightening. I was afraid that with my weight I would not be able to take off like my friends. But thankfully, I managed to keep up with them. Although we had all been fitted with life jackets, the fact that I was sailing through the air without any support under my feet was scary. I was initially afraid to open my eyes and appreciate the breathtaking view of the Goa coastline, but urged by Reema and Natasha, who I could hear shouting in joy, I opened them and the sight was overwhelming.

A good couple of hours went by before we decided to take a break to have tea and coffee at the Chocalatti. Then we headed out of Candolim for the Miramar beach that was considered to be prettier. We had been the noisiest lot here in Candolim as generally people came here to meditate, smoke pot or cozy up in the shacks. It was tailor made for that purpose.

At the Miramar beach, Natasha got her phone out of the bag, only to realise that there were three missed calls from Sandy. She called back only to discover that the mobile was switched off. Reema also checked her mobile and told us that there were five missed calls with messages to call back urgently; three were from Sandy and two from Amit. She read the messages in a perfunctory manner before placing her mobile back into her beach bag. Amit would be on the flight now and she didn't care to call Sandy back believing that he could have nothing urgent to share with her.

The stunning ambience of the beach captivated us completely. We laughed, ate ice cream and splashed water on each other as we walked along the shore. Reema made me run with her across the golden beach, as fast as our feet could take us. I collapsed on the sand finally and tried to catch my breath, but it was a great adrenaline rush. Meanwhile, Vick and Natasha were pining for lunch as it was well past 2 p.m.

At the Aguada, we ordered one bottle of Madera White and one Sula Sauvignon Blanc wine, whilst lazily feasting our eyes on the serene view outside; a slice of heaven that was naturally flawless. It was a truly spectacular beach with the Aguada Fort, built by the Portuguese in the 16th century, serving as the backdrop.

We were famished after all the activity at the beach and stuffed our faces with scrumptious sea food that Reema had ordered in abundance and even indulged on chips. Vick managed a sizeable portion of vegetarian food by himself and we chided him for missing out on the best of Goan culture.

After our meal, we just sat back to enjoy the idyllic setting, taking in the tranquility of the beach through all our senses. I had promised myself that I would visit the mosques nearby, but I was washed out with all the wine that I had consumed. It was 5 p.m. and we decided to head back to the hotel to take a nap before our evening plan.

Before that we thanked Reema from our hearts for initiating this plan and for giving us the opportunity to enjoy the trinity of sand, sea and sun. All three combined had a magical effect on our body, mind and spirits; we felt completely energised and rejuvenated as individuals.

It had been a much-needed getaway from the high-end society life of Delhi. Even Reema looked more relaxed. I was surprised that she had chosen to travel without all the bling that was so much a part of her personality. But I guess, she too could not ignore the lure of going back to her good old life with her good old friends, even if for a short period of time; much like the comfort of an old coat, over a brand new fur coat in the wardrobe. She was the happiest I had seen her, since my arrival in Delhi.

We clambered into a cab, chatting merrily all the way back to our hotel. The taxi driver was amused at our chirpiness and he too chitchatted with us, telling us about Goa and its various wonders.

27

All the wine that we had drunk wore off in a second. I watched as Reema, with unsteady hands, took the messages that had been left for us at the hotel.

'I'm very sorry Ma'am to give you this bad news...' said the receptionist.

We sprinted to our rooms, somehow threw all our stuff into our bags and headed straight back to the reception, where Reema stood like a stone with Vick clearing the bill and urging the receptionist to hurry with our bags. I ran back to Reema's room and packed all her things, doing a quick check of the bathroom. As I rushed back to the reception, the taxi driver was placing our stuff in the boot of the car. We jumped into it. Vick asked him to speed up to the airport. Reema told me to check her mobile for all the missed calls and messages. She did not have the courage to do so. The rest of us also checked our respective phones to find messages. This was probably the very first time that none of us had used our mobiles for the entire day — the reason why we had not learnt of Varun's accident till we reached the hotel.

Reema was trembling as we hurriedly checked in, went through security and sat in the lounge, waiting for an announcement on our flight. We sat in complete silence;

didn't know how to comfort Reema. I held onto her hand as Natasha and Vick brought her a bottle of packaged drinking water. We insisted that she have it. So far, there had been no reaction from her, but a stillness that was frightening. She just sat before us like a block of stone.

I noticed that the glow that I had seen on her face earlier had given way to a distraught expression. Vick sat next to her on the flight and Natasha and I could hear him reassuring her that all would be fine. How transient was life; one moment we were shedding tears of joy and the next moment there was sadness. This had to be the most traumatic time of Reema's life.

'I should have known, Vick,' she spoke out through tears. 'It's the first time I did not hear from my baby for hours. I should have realised that something was wrong; instead, I was busy having fun. How selfish of me... I should not have come to Goa.'

There were two cars waiting for us at the airport. A man in a smart suit waited with the cars. He reassured Reema that he would take care of everything and directed her to her C class Mercedes.

The driver pushed down the accelerator, gauging that she would want to reach her son as soon as possible, dodged the traffic lights, darted down some narrow lanes, which were shortcuts, passed some humble residential quarters and stores, then finally the plush malls of Saket to reach the Max Hospital, where her teenaged son lay fighting for his young life.

When we finally reached the corridor of the ICU, we noticed that the entire family was waiting outside. Sandy sat with his head bowed; grief-stricken and gaunt.

We were unprepared for Reema's reaction to him, 'It's all your f*****g fault you a*****e. Why couldn't you keep an eye on him in my absence? If anything happens to my son I will kill you and I mean it,' she screamed, while tugging at his shirt. She had almost hauled him to his feet in her anger.

Sandy remained surprisingly quiet, inspite of her assault; his swollen eyes indicating that he was exhausted from crying. Now they both stood staring at each other; trembling with both fear and anger.

The air was once again fraught with strain. The grandmother sat sombrely with her eyes closed, with prayer beads in her right hand as she appealed to the Gods in earnest, for her grandson's life. The grandfather looked frail as he sat holding onto his walking stick, his worry causing the creases on his forehead to deepen. Neither of them acknowledged Reema's presence. Not that she cared. They only cared for the grandchildren. Varun was their first grand-child; the apple of their eyes, their life. Arun sprinted towards his mom. He wrapped his hands around her waist and the two cried; he was the only person in the house she cared to share her grief with.

'The police are outside,' whispered Sandy, 'and the media is standing outside our house in Westend, waiting for the family's reaction. What should I do? This will be on the front page lines tomorrow morning. I need to handle this with care. It's a very delicate matter.'

Reema lashed out, 'You have been in many hot soups and have still come out of it dry, with the help of your scheming mind. It is only our lives that you couldn't sort out. That is why we are here in this hospital waiting to see what awaits us. You have made a hash of everything, absolutely everything Sandy, and I absolutely detest you. Now more than ever.'

She was beyond herself now in her anxiety and hate, 'And if Varun doesn't come out of his coma, I will destroy you before dumping you. I no longer care about this damned society and about keeping up appearances.'

Reema was now shaking like a leaf, with her eyes like piercing daggers, 'I have had enough of you. Do you hear me, ENOUGH!'

I realised that this was the moment of truth for Reema as she must surely realise that nothing mattered anymore; not her pretentious lifestyle, not her extravagant ways, nor her string of lovers.

She turned frantically towards Vick in the ICU, and asked, 'Why the hell are they not allowing me to see my son? I want to go inside.'

Vick reassured her that he would make an immediate enquiry, although Sandy had already told her that the doctor was in there examining him. He reminded her again and she shrieked in anger.

'Stay out of my way Sandy. I have been at the receiving end of all your rage, infidelity, manipulations and lies. My kids are the only thing precious to me. And now if I lose my son, I will make sure I wipe you out too.'

Natasha, Vick and I stood mute before her hostility. In a span of a few hours, we had seen her lose her bearing twice. But what we had witnessed in Goa was nothing compared to the expression on her face now as she spoke to Sandy and mowed him down with her hostility.

I wondered if it was the loss of fear that made her so strong in front of Sandy. She was on the verge of losing what was most precious to her; she didn't care how Sandy would react to her now.

Reema glanced over at her parents-in-law and their worried faces and wondered if she should console them but she had always blamed them for not intervening to reprimand Sandy for his ways. She hadn't cared about them for too long a period to make the show of being polite to them.

Turning towards the ICU, she tried to look through the sliver of a window at her son in bandages, and with tears in her eyes cried out, in whispers, 'Wake up Varun! I love you and I need you baby. I promise you, it will all be different now. Please wake up! Please baby! I will be a good mother to you. Just give me another chance. Oh God please! Where did I go wrong?'

We encouraged Reema to sit down until the doctors left the intensive care and she could go see her unconscious son. But she was visibly frightened and fidgety and preferred to pace up and down the corridor. Finally she sat down by herself at the far end of the corridor, away from all of us.

Vick and I fetched coffee for her and a bottle of packaged drinking water but she didn't want any, although her lips appeared parched.

She just sat with her head lowered, staring vacantly at the impeccably polished floor of the hospital. She was pale and looked exhausted, as if 20 years had been added to her youthful face. Her eyes had lost the usual sparkle.

Natasha expressed the desire to return to the Bangla Sahib Gurudwara to pray for Varun. Reema's eyes sparkled for a moment and she nodded, giving her approval. Natasha rang some of her cousins, requesting them to accompany her and they came to the hospital to fetch her. She looked at Reema intently before she left, as though assuring her to hold on till she took her prayers to the Gurudwara.

I had never seen Natasha like this before. I shared her fear for Varun and the possibility that if something were to happen to him, then Reema and Sandy's marriage would fall apart completely. Even for the sake of appearances they would not be able to stay together. What would happen to Reema then?

Vick and I decided to stick on with Reema as a few close relatives were walking in to enquire about Varun.

A few minutes after Natasha left, a young girl walked into the private waiting area to quietly sit next to Reema. She put her arms around her and held her tight. Reema was surprised, but it did not take her long to recognise that this was the girl her boy had fallen for. I, of course, had seen her before with Varun. Reema responded to the comfort that the girl offered and held onto her, perhaps praying that their young love would be strong enough to bring her Varun back.

The girl had a calm demeanour that affected each one of us, who had been standing there under great stress. I hoped that her sincerity would ensure that they have a happy and fulfilling life, although they were too young to contemplate ever after. But it was certainly refreshing in a generation that didn't have the patience to persevere in relationships.

Our generation danced to Tina Turner's song 'What's Love Got To Do With It.' When I first heard it I remember feeling sad at the possibility of love fading into insignificance in relationships, but today's generation has adopted to this practical way of thinking without batting an eyelid. But then why just blame them. My generation that once proclaimed the eternity of love was now making a mockery of this emotion in their relationships.

It seemed like Arun had met her before as he inched towards her to ask if he could borrow her mobile to call home and ask if Cleo was doing fine. It was probably his way of dealing with the fear of what he might have to face.

Vick quickly detected the look of fear and helplessness in the little one's eyes and walked over to sit beside him.

'How you doing buddy? Your brother is going to be out of here in no time, you know that right?' reassured Vick.

Arun responded without hesitation, 'He better be, because if he isn't then I'll run away with Cleo to another country. I won't live with mama and papa. I love them but I don't like the way they behave. Cleo and I don't like the way they fight and scream at each other — they never stop. They should get divorced.'

Vick and I looked at each other. What did he know about divorce?

Arun added, 'My friend's parents got divorced. He used to tell me that they would always yell at each other, like mama and papa…'

'They both love you and your brother very much Arun,' Vick interrupted. 'Grown-ups can be confusing at times, but they mean well buddy? Once Varun comes around we can help them sort things out. They really adore both of you. Trust me on this. I would never lie to you; after all, you and I are buddies.'

'Yes! I know that! I like you Vick uncle, but I know that papa doesn't. Oops! I wasn't supposed to tell you that. I'm sorry.'

Vick just smiled tenderly as he noticed an unmistakable twinkle in Arun's eyes. Kids were so perceptive, and yet so innocent. He wasn't sure whether Sandy would like having him around, but he was here for Reema and her boys. He didn't care what Sandy thought of him.

'Cleo gets very upset when mama and papa fight. He is the only one who has time for me in the house. Mama is always running. She doesn't really have time for me,' said Arun with his head lowered, sadness in his eyes.

'She always tells me that she'll take me for a movie and bowling at Blue O but then someone calls and she changes the plan. She tells me she really loves me. I sometimes feel that she is lying to me. My friend's mama always takes him out and wants to spend time with him. She actually loves her son. I don't think mama actually loves me Vick uncle. She just pretends.'

'Hey buddy, why don't you and I make plans for a movie and bowling on a weekend? Better still, we will wait till Varun gets home and then plan something.'

The little one smiled, probably sensing the sincerity in Vick's voice.

28

The police approached Sandy at the hospital, for an inquiry, disregarding the sensitivity of the situation. Vick noticed the anxiety on Sandy's face and immediately rushed to his side. I had been sitting with Sandy's parents. The arrival of the police might distress Arun, so I ensured that he was with me. Reema was in no state to be a support to somebody else, even if it was her own son. He was insisting on going home as he felt that Cleo must be wondering what was going on. Sandy had earlier sent his driver to fetch the maid, so that she could take care of Arun.

Sandy had been anticipating the arrival of the police. I had overheard him talk to somebody on the phone earlier; to some influential person perhaps. From what I could gauge of the conversation he had been advised not to evade the enquiry.

He had understood the importance of being civil, 'It happened at around 4 a.m. I came home after a bash at a friend's place and went into the bedroom of each of the boys, as I usually do, to check on them. Arun was fast asleep but Varun's bed was empty. At first I thought he had stayed over at a friend's place and he must've informed Reema, as he usually does. I was in Mumbai yesterday and I was to fly to Goa as I had promised Reema's friends that I would join them there. But I received an important business call from Delhi so I had to return here.'

'When did you get back from Mumbai?' asked the inspector.

'I returned yesterday, late afternoon, but I didn't inform Reema's friends about this. It was meant to be a surprise for Reema but then business took over as it usually does. Even then I didn't see Varun when I returned home after work and before heading for the party, but that was not unusual as we tend to be busy with our respective things.

'A white Porche Cayenne finally rolled up at 4:30 a.m. and Cleo rushed downstairs, wagging his tail in anticipation. I too followed him but with a feeling of uneasiness as it was odd for anyone to visit us at that unearthly hour. But then I thought it must be Varun. I knew something was seriously wrong when Micky, Varun's friend, came out of his car looking totally distraught.

'Arun, my younger one, sprinted out onto the driveway. He too had heard the sound of the car. The maid followed. He was frantic when Micky broke the news of the accident.'

I was looking at Sandy as he spoke to the police inspector, trying desperately to maintain his composure. He was obviously under a lot of stress, as he imagined the worst for his son. His urbane charm had vanished and what radiated from him was only fear. Exhaustion and worry had robbed him of his youthful looks. If Sandy looked old, his parents certainly appeared worse. As Sandy glanced at them to reassure them, after the arrival of the inspector, I wondered how they would handle it if the worst were to happen.

Vick politely requested the inspector if he could postpone the enquiry until Varun gained consciousness, as the family was under unfathomable strain.

'I really want to keep this matter away from public eye,' urged Sandy in a trembling voice. 'We don't know, at this point, if my son is ever going to talk again. He may never come out of his coma. Please inspector we need our privacy.' Putting the worst situation into words seemed to snap something inside him and he broke down, crying like a defenceless boy.

Vick held him while he cried and I wondered if those tears may have been shed for more reasons than was acknowledged — perhaps Varun's accident was going to be a wake-up call for both Reema and Sandy. They would perhaps realise the importance of being a family.

For Sandy this was also a revelation of another kind; for the first time in his life perhaps he had no control over the situation he was in. He could not do anything to pull Varun out of the dark dreary woods. For a man who did not believe in the power of the Almighty, this was definitely a very helpless situation.

'I'm very sorry Mr. Mehra,' responded the inspector while ensuring that his tone was soft. 'I do understand the situation and completely empathise with you, but the media is already outside your residence. This is the case of a stolen

Ferrari, as well as cocaine that your son has already been tested for. Your residence is once again under scrutiny for narcotics, as it was some years back.' It was apparent that the police inspector was very well aware of Sandy's status in society; especially his connections at the top. Hence, he was careful not to threaten him, but was gently communicating the charges his family would be facing.

29

Minutes ticked by as we waited outside the ICU.

I looked at Arun and realised that he must be tired and hungry. So I took him down to the hospital canteen. While he settled down with his *pav bhaji*, I too indulged in some stress eating with a plate of hot *aloo paranthas*.

We were both on the heavy side and although I was sure that he would soon go from fat to flat, as he was still very young, his mother would make sure that he hit the gym and see a nutritionist before he turned 16.

While devouring the food, and temporarily forgetting his worries as he loved eating, Arun spoke in a soft voice, 'Zoya aunty, can I ask you something?'

'Of course Arun! Anything!' I responded.

'Zoya aunty, can you tell mama to leave papa, for my sake please, because I know that Varun *Bhaiya* is sick because of them. I too will fall sick if they stay together. I'm getting a headache with all this,' he said as he touched his head to demonstrate. 'Cleo doesn't even ack... ack... I don't remember that word mama taught me.'

'Acknowledge?' I offered, while polishing off my comfort food. 'Cleo doesn't acknowledge whom? Your mom and dad?'

'That's right Zoya aunty. Cleo is very intelligent and knows that mama and papa are not behaving right. Mama comes to my PTA meetings and while she is hurriedly talking to my teachers she is busy with her mobile. Later, she scolds me for not doing well in a subject when the teacher had told her that I was doing well. She is not even listening. She just doesn't care.'

I could see the dejection in his eyes.

I was left speechless as I had thought that Reema was a good mother, even if everything else in her life was far from perfect. Not being honest to the needs of the children did not give her much credibility as a mother. She needed to prioritise what was really important in her life.

The Reema I knew in the '80s was always a go-getter, but always for things that made her better; she strived to be the best version of herself, to unleash her potential and to live the most fulfilling life. She was admirably an all-rounder who had a clear thinking and was intelligent. I felt sorry that somehow she had lost the plot.

As I watched Arun's chubby fingers feed his red D&G T-shirt more than his mouth, I hoped that Natasha was not only praying for Varun's life, at the Gurudwara, but also for Reema, so that she could steer her life in the right direction. And for Sandy too, to rediscover the love he once had for his wife. Arun especially was too young to understand how his little world was on the verge of crumbling.

I was once again reminded of his innocence and couldn't help but smile as I saw that he had put more food in his mouth than he could chew. He appeared far too exhausted now to eat. Finally, he left some of it on the plate and insisted that I pack it for Cleo, who must be hungry and was surely missing him. He wanted to go back home soon to be with the only one who loved him genuinely.

30

Vick had not left Sandy's side since the episode with the police inspector. When I returned from the canteen I saw the two seated on the chairs outside Varun's ICU. Reema was sitting where I had seen her last. She probably would not move till her son woke up, I told myself. She was resting her head against the wall behind her and her eyes were closed.

I did not want to disturb her, so I walked over to Vick and Sandy, as Arun told the maid that he wanted to go to the toilet.

When I reached them, I realised that Sandy was talking about the accident.

'You know what, Vick, the red Ferrari belonged to my friend, Kenny Kohli, or KK as he is called by his acquaintances. It was smashed; totally and irreparably smashed. KK does not forgive easily. A rich businessman, he can be pretty ruthless and is known for his high-profile links.'

Sandy continued with a voice that I now noticed had a slight tremble. He told Vick that KK, his so-called buddy, had filed a case against him. And since he had more political connections, it would be difficult to extricate himself from the case.

'He was the first to buy a Bentley and a Lamborghini, and even an Aston Martin, and has a fleet of the latest models of ultra luxury cars lined up in his farm in Western Greens, and that includes a Porsche Cayenne, a Mercedes Benz and a BMW convertible. He even owns a private jet. The size of his possessions is larger than the size of his heart. And he will not forgive my son for destroying his possession,' said Sandy sadly, as if he was speaking to himself.

He looked at Vick, perhaps realising that he too had been judgmental of Vick. And this time when he spoke his eyes revealed his deep remorse, 'Vick, I got you all wrong buddy and I owe you an apology for that. You are a good guy and I should have been more respectful to you.'

'It's all cool Sandy,' said Vick, in his usual affable way.

I was impressed that Vick could dismiss Sandy's earlier attitude so easily. But then Vick was a gem of a person, in a society that didn't really value people as much as it did its precious stones.

'Vick, I need to take you into confidence. I didn't give the entire story to the inspector. Micky, Varun's friend told me everything. There was a rave party at KK's place that was hosted by his son, Amir, and his classmate, Aditya. The kids got high on cocaine and ecstasy. There was also abundance of booze, as expected. The boys and girls had occupied the rooms at the farm. They were obviously having sex.

'Kenny and his wife were staying at their Delhi home for the weekend and had granted their son, Amir, permission to throw a party. They gave their consent in good faith, as most parents do, and didn't bother to check on what the kids were up to.

'Anyway, after a few hours, I am told, Amir began bragging to his friends, particularly the girls, about the flashy cars his father owned. He commanded the guards to open the garage and then hand over the keys of some of the cars as he wanted to show his friends the interiors of the vehicles.' Sandy's voice broke as he conveyed what had happened next.

'Varun was under the influence of booze, mixed with whatever... I don't know. Perhaps it was weed or something stronger; heaven knows. He sat in the Ferrari for fun and one of the girls challenged him to drive it even as she sat next to him. Varun apparently said that he was going to drive it on a clear stretch of road that was the Delhi-Agra expressway. Micky discouraged him sensing the danger.

'Varun abused him and told him to stop being such a spoilsport. The drivers too were terribly anxious and advised Amir to stop Varun. But they too were ignored.'

Sandy's voice choked, 'They found him on the national highway; luckily close to the farm. He must have swerved hard, lost control and hit the side barrier. It's a wonder that they both came out in one piece. The girl is injured but not critical. My boy may be on his last breath and I believe I may be responsible for that. It was my reckless lifestyle that my boy imitated. Reema doesn't know but I allowed him to drive our cars when she wasn't around; even though he is under-age. In a sense I taught him the art of lying and that's why none of us knew about him attending a rave party.'

Just then Vick's phone rang. It was Natasha. He listened intently before turning to Sandy. 'Sandy, your home is surrounded by the media. Cameras have been set up at the entrance. Not to mention the curious neighbours who are also crowding the gates. They are all waiting for the story.'

'Story!' yelled Sandy. 'Is that what this has been reduced to — a story? Varun is my son, not a goddamn story. Tell the buggers to get out of there before I shoot them all.'

'Sandy, we will battle it out. What's most important is that we must pray for Varun's health. The rest will fall into place. You know Sandy, my mom always says that when the intent is pure then God comes down to help his children,' said Vick with all conviction.

Standing nearby, I was horrified of what I had overheard. But I was more surprised at what I heard next.

Sandy turned to Vick, 'Vick, I don't know what to do. But I do need to go home to Westend to see what's going on. Will you come with me?'

Sandy had clearly found a new respect for Vick.

Inspite of all that I had heard about him from Reema, my heart ached for Sandy. The very society that he worked so hard to gel into was not there for him in his hour of need; they were never there, but he just didn't see it then.

31

'There is very little chance of your son coming out of his coma; I am very sorry Sandy. We have done all that we could. Now God needs to show mercy,' reported doctor Mehta, who was also a friend of the family.

Natasha had returned to the hospital and both of us turned to Reema. There was a stunned expression on her face and she brushed us aside as we reached out to her.

She just sat on a chair beside Varun's bed and gently, but firmly, held his limp hand.

'Varun I love you. Please come home to mama baby... Please don't leave mama. I know you can hear every word, my baby. I am hurting right now for all that I haven't done for you, or for that matter even for your baby brother. Your dad and I have had problems and chose my own way to deal with them. I knew no better son. But I somehow lost my way in the wilderness; foolishly trading all that matters for that which doesn't.

'I know that we are a far from perfect family. But we love you. I hope you can find it in your heart... to forgive your foolish mother, baby... please.'

Reema broke down as she said the words and rested her head on Varun's abdomen as he lay there in deep slumber.

'Oh God! Please listen to me... I am so sorry for everything that I have done wrong. Please let my son come back to me.'

She cried and cried and so did Natasha and I, as we decided to enter the ICU to support her. Natasha placed her hand on her shoulder as I took a chair and sat next to her.

Sometimes hours can feel like minutes, but today minutes felt like a lifetime as we waited for a sign of life.

It was late and we were advised to leave. Reema however refused to budge. Sandy came into the ICU.

'I know you despise me Reema and you don't want to hear this but you have to go home and rest. You need to be okay so that you can pray for him. Please Reema.' He was trying to get through to her. I noticed the hesitation in his voice. Too much had gone wrong between them and he knew that.

But perhaps the shared concern for their son would help to bridge the gap to a certain extent. I fervently hoped it would.

But Reema just ignored him.

The hours just ticked by and we waited.

Sandy's mother had not stopped praying even for a minute. She put away her prayer beads only to pick up the *Hanuman Chalisa*. Sandy's father just sat quietly. There was fatigue in their bodies but their heart and mind overcame that as they continued to pray for Varun.

Reema's head was still resting on Varun's abdomen and her hand held onto his. Sandy now sat on the other side of the bed. We decided to wait outside; to give the family some space.

Just as we were leaving, Arun entered the ICU.

There was a strange conviction in his voice as he spoke, 'Varun *Bhaiya*! Wake up now. You've been sleeping for too long. Wake up and don't worry about mama and papa because they are getting divorced just like my friend's parents. You don't have to live with them anymore. If you want we will also divorce them both.'

Reema lifted her head up and stared at Arun in bewilderment. Sandy too sat up straight.

'Varun *Bhaiya*, Cleo, you and I will leave the country. You are going to study in the US next year and I'll go with you. Cleo and I don't want to hear mama and papa shouting at each other.'

I noticed Sandy and Reema's eyes meet across Varun's bed. They were both trying to check the stream of tears running down their cheeks.

And then the miracle happened.

Varun's hand twitched and Sandy rushed to caress his son's face while Reema waited with bated breath just staring at him. Arun was the only one who stood there with a calm expression on his face.

Varun opened his eyes slowly.

'Thank God! Thank God!' was all Sandy could say as Reema wept tears of gratitude. For somebody, who did not believe in God, Sandy's words took us all by surprise.

Varun's recovery did something amazing for his parents. For the first time since our arrival, we saw the two holding hands in joy.

Would they be able to rebuild what they had lost?

For today at least the Mehras were a picture of supreme bliss as they laughed together. Their family had been saved.

Epilogue

Sandy's farm had never looked more stunning. The sparkle of the décor was almost as much as the stars shining down on all of us. The moon also shone in its full silvery grandeur. Our hearts were beating to the foot-tapping music that pulsated every inch of the place. The guests wore their best; both in terms of attire and attitude. Natasha and I had never witnessed such a spectacular party before.

The Ferrari car accident had hit the headlines, but none of Sandy and Reema's friends had asked uncomfortable questions. Perhaps this was a rare show of sensitivity or they just didn't care. Who cared in a society that was inundated with scandals anyway?

Varun's accident and its repercussions on Sandy's friendship with KK would soon fade into insignificance. The case would go on and Sandy would be fighting it single-handedly without the support of his fair-weather friends. In the meanwhile, Sandy would continue to host brilliant bashes as he had done tonight and they would all be beside him again in their own Ferraris. Sandy's latest silver GT V8 Bentley had arrived and was brought onto the lawns; to be flaunted before his VIP guests, who applauded at its arrival. We watched as four stunningly slender models in skimpy black leotards stepped out seductively from each door of the car and then dragged Sandy inside it. Onlookers shouted in excitement as he revved up the engine to show off its power that was almost akin to his own.

Natasha and I had our own reason to be happy at this party — we had bought a new ensemble each from a celebrated Indian designer, who was also amongst Reema's guests. In addition, we had bought an LV bag each. The brand bug had finally bitten us.

Reema looked her usual striking self in a silver sequined dress that enhanced her slender figure, Dolce and Gabbana silver sequined clutch and Jimmy Choo shoes. She was a vision tonight. With her diamond jewellery and solitaire ring, that Sandy had gifted her, she was the lady of the night enthralling everyone with her shimmering presence. In fact everything that glittered tonight was either gold or diamond and nothing less. Every being and object shone bright like the diamonds in the sky.

But I had also noticed a change in her. She was watching over Varun more than her guests. The young boy was recovering well and had invited his girlfriend, Daisy, to the party.

Amit was also present at the party; I once again marveled at his good looks and noticed the way his eyes followed Reema sometimes. I was sure that even Reema's heart beat faster at the sight of him. But she would not give him any special attention today; Sandy and she were the hosts tonight and so every guest would get the same amount of attention. Amit and Reema's relationship was complex and there was no way of knowing, at this stage, if it was something that was for keeps. For the time being, though, it was lust as usual for them.

But Varun's accident had also brought something back into Reema and Sandy's marriage; it had reminded them of their responsibility as parents among other things.

Earlier, I had noticed Arun sitting on the first floor terrace with Cleo, who was wearing a silver Dolce & Gabbana collar. Together they watched the glittering party. He adjusted his silver bow tie that all the four men in the family were wearing that evening; that included Grandfather. Grandmother wore a silver saree that made her look ever so graceful. She also wore a smile of gratitude for having her grandson return to her.

The older members of the family had chosen to spend the evening in the quieter part of the house. Reema had thoughtfully invited some of their acquaintances; the first time in years that she had made an effort for Sandy's parents, she told Natasha, Vick and me on an aside.

After Sandy had shown off his new toy on four wheels, he offered rose champagne, to his guests, as an aperitif. He then served Blue Label to the ladies who cherished their scotch. Dalmore 62 was ostentatiously displayed at the bar. Vick had told us that he had paid a fortune for it at an auction the previous year. Nothing succeeds like excess. Sandy's glass was always full and tonight it was spilling over with the joy of getting his son back; in fact, that was the real cause of celebration tonight. His laughter, I noticed, sounded sincere, much like the Sandy we knew earlier.

Sandy took Varun, his girlfriend, Daisy, and Arun to sit in his new car. His eyes searched around and we realised that he was looking for Reema. We then saw her escorting Sandy's parents to where her husband and boys awaited her.

As the evening wore on, the tempo of the party started picking up pace. Young striking ladies hung around, alluring in their skimpy and almost non-existent dresses. They were as available as the rose champagne. Stronger stuff was available, but would be offered once Sandy's parents with their friends and the boys turned in for the night.

The Moulin Rouge performance came on at midnight and after a spectacular performance that left the guests spellbound, music, Hindi and English mix, filled the exuberant air. The dance floor was packed in no time with men and women dancing seductively and most energetically.

Natasha was dancing with one of the guests with unbridled joy; this time her partner was a good-looking man with eyes that weren't leering at her but gazing at her with admiration. She had dressed her best tonight; even got her teeth whitened by Reema's dishy dentist. She had plenty to smile about as she had all intentions of hooking up with her dance partner either here in the party or later at Reema's farm, I concluded in amusement.

Vick, looking dapper in a black ensemble, stood by me as we wondered whether we should hit the dance floor ourselves. He looked happy and had just shared the good news that Sandy would be assisting him for the license for the restaurant he had been planning for quite some time; their plan finally was set to fructify by the end of the year. I promised him that I would return for its grand opening. We soaked in the magical aura of Reema and Sandy's 25th wedding anniversary at their most ornately and opulently dressed up farm. We wondered if they would both stand under the gazebo that had been exquisitely and exorbitantly adorned by the leading florist in Delhi who embellished most wedding and social parties. I momentarily envisioned them holding hands and kissing each other tenderly.

I was practically jolted out of my daydreaming as Natasha shook me by the shoulder to point out that Rohit had entered the party, this time alone. Vick nudged me to go and open the closed, but not locked, door of his heart.

Rohit and I danced under the moonlight with my heart and mind dizzy with excitement. Reema had made me buy a pair of comfortable silver Gucci shoes for tonight, and I didn't need to take it off all night.

'As clichéd as it may sound, you've never looked more lovely. It's only after you left that I realised how deep my love for you was,' Rohit said as he held me closer and then he whispered into my ear, 'I shouldn't have let you go to London, Zoya. We only value the person once they have turned their backs on us.'

I could feel my heart beating loudly. I was as excited as a teenager would be having her true love reciprocate her feelings; happiness surged through every cell of my body.

Reema's party had created the perfect setting for me to voice my feelings. I felt beautiful and considered myself the happiest woman in the world.

I whispered to him, 'Marry me Rohit. Time is running out for all of us and I want to be happy for the rest of my years.' I said, with tears of joy welling up in my eyes.

Rohit laughed aloud and then with his eyes dancing in amusement, said, 'Go down on your knees and offer me the latest Bentley and a Versace wardrobe... then I shall consider your proposal. My standards are a little out of the ordinary... if you know what I mean...'

I pushed him away teasingly before he pulled me back to him and whispered. 'I love you and always have and I want nothing more than to have you with me for the rest of my life... that, and your sexy body, I don't need anything.'

I laughed aloud and one again lost myself in the warmth of his embrace.

Happiness had sneaked into my life through the door that I didn't know I had left unlocked.

Enrique Iglesias came on to perform at two in the morning and swept everyone off their feet. Reema and Amit audaciously danced to 'Tonight I'm Loving You.' Everyone looks for perfect love; In fact it is the perennial search of every human being. Sandy then danced with one of the models to 'Dirty Dancer.' Both the men and women cheered breathlessly as Enrique sang and danced spiritedly to all his top numbers. He asked some of the women guests to join him on stage. My heart skipped a beat as he pointed at me. It was by far the most exciting moment of my life as I wriggled my hips as he looked into my eyes.

At just past three, Reema and Sandy cut their six-tiered anniversary cake. It was covered in white icing, with silver ribbons to match the silver bows on each elegantly dressed table and chair at the venue. Even as they cut the cake, the girls serving cocktails and champagne, in silver bikinis, released silver balloons, with initials *R* and *S,* that glided up towards the starlit skies.

Enrique filled the air with 'Hero,' as his finale song and I noticed Sandy and Reema momentarily gaze into each other's eyes with what seemed like love.

I told myself that the two may just be able to bridge the distance between them. After having gone through such agonising heartache, would love find a way back? Or would they part ways after tonight or perhaps they would continue with their marriage of convenience, except now in a more civil tone.

The party rocked all night long with Delhi decidedly singing alongside Rihanna's 'We Found Love In A Hopeless Place,' followed by 'Don't Stop The Music.'

The revelers at the party may not stick up for each other but they did stick to each other while they concluded the night dancing and singing to Bollywood queen Kareena Kapoor's popular number, 'Fevicol Se.'